SOFT SERVE

T0243940

SOFT SERVE

stories

ALLISON GRAVES

BREAKWATER
P.O. Box 2188, St. John's, NL, Canada, A1C 6E6
WWW.BREAKWATERBOOKS.COM

COPYRIGHT © 2023 Allison Graves
FRONT COVER PHOTOGRAPH © Ethan Murphy

Library and Archives Canada Cataloguing in Publication
Title: Soft serve / Allison Graves.
Names: Graves, Allison, author.
Identifiers: Canadiana 20230182607 | ISBN 9781550819861 (softcover)
Classification: LCC PS8613.R38245 S64 2023 | DDC C813/.6—dc23

We acknowledge the support of the Canada Council for the Arts.
We acknowledge the financial support of the Government of Canada
through the Department of Heritage and the Government of Newfoundland and Labrador through the Department of Tourism, Culture,
Arts and Recreation for our publishing activities.

PRINTED AND BOUND IN CANADA.

 Canada Council Conseil des arts   Canada   Newfoundland
for the Arts du Canada   Labrador

Breakwater Books is committed to choosing papers and materials for
our books that help to protect our environment. To this end, this book
is printed on recycled paper that is certified by the Forest Stewardship
Council®.

For my parents

CONTENTS

1   Ceiling like the Sky

8   Eat Me

21   Shallow Water

37   Sugar

43   My Friend, My Parrot

53   IKEA Showroom

57   Soft Serve

71   Bad Ending

81   Value

96   Stand By

108   Winter Salad

121   Flat Circle

129   Swiffer WetJet

138   Halfway Somewhere

153   Staying Alive

167   Undeclared

170   It's Getting Dark Out

183   No Man's Land

204   Stars

CEILING LIKE THE SKY

One hundred centimetres of snow fell and our house was completely buried. I lived in a cold and winding house in downtown St. John's with three other girls. Grace was on vacation with her family in Thailand and kept sending us videos of her on the beach sipping drinks with umbrellas in them. We told her to stop but she insisted.

The first day wasn't so bad—Franny got really high off a preroll she'd bought from the Tweed store on Water Street and kept reminding us how smart she was for getting weed before the storm. She convinced Lily to share a preroll and Lily started hyperventilating while we watched *Drag Race*. She was losing her mind thinking about how we had no way out and kept telling me that if it came down to it—because my room was only a couple feet from the top of the snowbank— that I would have to jump out the window and start digging. I told her I would, but that didn't regulate her breathing.

I worked at a restaurant downtown and was sleeping on and off with my boss, Rick, who had been my best friend for years. He messaged me first thing after the snowfall saying he slipped a disc shovelling and understood why we were anxious because he would have to spend the next week horizontal. I told him it wasn't exactly the same but he said it was close. His girlfriend, Courtney, was at her parents' house helping them shovel out and Rick was concerned about how he would fill up his Nalgene.

Anytime something didn't work out with someone he was dating, Rick would come back to me. He understood that I loved him and wanted to be together but would remind me every time that the stakes were too high—I was too important for him to lose. His dishonesty and flimsiness of character were traits I saw regularly but ignored. It was like I was ski racing and I was getting hit in the face by the red flags over and over again but I just kept going. The girls in the house were unanimous in thinking that Rick had been treating me like shit for years. I'd had frank conversations with them about it before and I would listen to their advice and then would completely exhaust them by ignoring the advice they gave. I could feel myself doing this and it made me feel embarrassed, but that didn't make me stop.

Franny started making cookies and tidying up the living room. Then she rolled out a pie dough while the oven was preheating and I could tell that she was high as a kite. Franny was probably the most anxious one of all of us, but she could hide it when she wanted to.

"I think we should watch all the UK *Love Island* starting at Season One," Franny yelled from the kitchen.

"We've already seen them all," Lily replied. "But the first two are actually so great 'cause they're more real—it's before they started like censoring all their behaviour."

"I'm down," I said. "I think it's going to be at least until tomorrow before someone can dig us out."

Lily's phone rang and it was Grace FaceTiming us from

Thailand. Grace's sisters were in the background and they were all fighting. Grace was clearly drunk because her eyes were glassy and her cheeks were red. I thought she looked pretty.

"I wish I was there with you guys!" she said. "This is so shit —nothing interesting ever happens in town and I leave and you guys get three days off work trapped in the house."

"We're starting *Love Island* from Season One!" Franny yelled from the kitchen as her timer went off.

"Oh my God, you guys—those are my favourite seasons!"

When we hung up Lily said she wished Grace was there and that something didn't feel right without her. We started watching *Love Island* until it got dark out and I felt slightly panicked that I couldn't leave the situation even if I wanted to. We had finished Franny's cookies and I was desperate for a walk. Rick was messaging me about how he was having a Cronenberg marathon with Courtney and I swear I could have barfed right there and then.

"I don't know, we don't even really talk anymore," Rick texted about Courtney. "It's like we're existing on different planets or something."

I didn't respond but he could see that I'd read the message.

"I don't know, she really wants kids. And I told her I could never do that."

I told Lily and Franny that I was going to the bathroom and I went upstairs and sobbed into my pillow until I heard the *Love Island* theme song downstairs signalling the beginning of a new episode. I grabbed my phone from where I'd left it on my desk and I had eleven missed messages from Rick all saying "I'm sorry" and asking if that was too much information and how sometimes he didn't know how to navigate our relationship.

"Sorry, I don't want you to feel like I'm a shitty guy . . . you're so important to me. Really I don't know what I would do without you."

I messaged him back and told him it was fine. "Sorry, we're watching *Love Island* and it's seriously insane. I feel like my brain is getting mushy lol."

When I came downstairs my face was red and Franny looked at me and knew I was upset but didn't ask. My relationship with Rick had been hardest on Franny. She'd been there since the start and she understood every contour of it. Franny was the type of person who believed that when she gave advice, people were going to take it. And each time I ignored her and put myself in a position to get hurt, Franny moved slightly further away from me. I could feel it. Each time I tried to explain by telling her I was a control freak and these things weren't as easy for me as they were for her. I told her she was freer than I was. This time she didn't ask, though.

I had weird dreams all night that I couldn't remember in the morning and I blamed *Love Island*. When I came down the stairs the next morning, Franny was watching *Videodrome* on the TV in the living room and had hung up the wool blankets I had collected since childhood on the large windows so as not to let the light in.

"Rick told me he was watching this last night. He's having a Cronenberg marathon," I said as I sat down on the couch she wasn't using.

"That's cool."

"I was having these weird dreams all night. I think the contrast between like *Love Island* and Snowmageddon has my brain all twisted," I said, biting my thumbnail so short it was painful. "Did you know all these *Love Island* contestants keep killing themselves? It's all so eerie."

"Dude, can you just let me watch this? It's almost done."

"All right, fine," I said.

I went upstairs and called my mom and told her Franny had pinned my nice blankets to the wall and it made me upset. My mom told me she was worried and detailed some of the crazy storms she'd lived through growing up in Newfoundland.

"Remember what happened to your cousin in Grand Falls? He was out playing in the snow when he was four years old and a snowplow buried him. He was under there for over an hour. And he was fine—I guess he had a little air pocket or something he was breathing through."

"Jesus," I said, even though I knew my mom didn't like it when I used that language.

"This is why I get scared, sweets. You guys have to be careful getting out of your house. Your father and I were watching *Here and Now* and they called in the army to plow the highways, baby."

I promised her we would be careful and that we were fine. I went back downstairs and Franny was at the part of the movie where the videotape is coming out of James Woods's abdomen. The whole thing made me feel hungry.

When Lily came downstairs it was almost noon and she told us that she'd been in her room watching anime and drawing. "I Googled *snowmageddon* and it said that *snowpocalypse* and *snowzilla* are also words the press uses to describe storms of massive proportions," she said. "Isn't that funny?"

That's when Franny complained she was running low on weed because she'd smoked so much yesterday and she'd binge-eaten too many cookies and was feeling unbelievably bloated. She said she missed her boyfriend Ross, who was doing a PhD in Toronto, and she felt alone and scared and trapped. She said she couldn't hear me talk about Rick any more without losing her mind and that *Love Island* and *Videodrome* and the steady stream of Snowmageddon photos on Instagram had made her brain feel fucked. She said she wanted to do something productive because it was the first time she'd had a few days off work but she couldn't concentrate on anything so she'd bought a small top with strings you wrap around the back from Aritzia for 120 dollars.

I reminded her she would never wear a top like that in town and she started crying and said, "I know okay," so loudly it almost bounced off the walls.

"I need to get out of here," she said between laboured breaths. "Someone needs to get us out of here." I knew she meant the house but I thought something bigger was going on. I wanted to be a better friend to her but I was barely hanging on myself. I wanted to tell her about my cousin surviving in the air pocket after getting buried with snow but I didn't think it would help.

Lily's boyfriend Jonathan came to dig us out that afternoon and three other neighbours pitched in to help. I watched them from my bedroom window and was happy I hadn't tried to jump. Jonathan created a tunnel to the road and we kept it that way for a week because it was funny.

The day after we were freed, Rick asked me if I wanted to go to the Golden Phoenix on Kenmount for all-you-can-eat buffet. At this point we had talked so much since the comment about him and Courtney having kids that I'd convinced him—

and maybe myself—that it was all okay. The drive to Golden Phoenix in Rick's Corolla was dicey at best and we slid for half a block coming down Freshwater. When we got there I had more food than I'd had in ages and chalked it up to a scarcity mindset given rationing while the city was shut down.

"I think Franny's mad at me," I told Rick as I shoved a chicken ball in my mouth in one bite.

"Franny's a bit temperamental. She'll be okay," Rick said.

I thought it was rich that he would be calling anyone else temperamental but I didn't say anything. I just made an mmm sound like I agreed with him. "How was the Cronenberg marathon after?"

"It was all right. Courtney got grossed out when the guy's head explodes in *Scanners* so she made me turn on something else."

I laughed and secretly wished he would stop talking to me about Courtney.

"I don't know, she just doesn't really understand or appreciate body horror," Rick said. He had some red sauce by his mouth and it looked like blood almost. "Did you ever notice if you look up at the ceiling here it's painted like the sky?"

I looked up and appreciated it for what felt like minutes. The gold light fixtures hung down in the middle of the sky.

"I think it's kind of beautiful," Rick said.

"Really?" I lowered my head and looked at him. "It makes me feel trapped."

EAT ME

Miranda was studying Bill Clinton's erections for a critical theory class: when he got it up and when he went soft. She wanted to make an argument about what it means to be presidential and if you have to be hard. She was doing a master's degree in social anthropology at the University of Toronto and working at a coffee shop with no Wi-Fi where you needed a key to open the washroom. Her boss told her it was trendy not to have Wi-Fi. She said it made people concentrate and think outside of the internet. Miranda thought her boss was annoying on Facebook but she didn't tell her that.

Miranda was dating a woman named Sasha who was making large light installations for a show at the Cooper Cole. The show also incorporated a performance where Sasha sucked on lightbulbs of different wattages while people moved through the gallery. When Miranda asked why, Sasha shrugged her shoulders and said it had to do with power and relationships and electricity.

Sasha's performance at Nuit Blanche had recently been profiled in *Canadian Art*, which called her one of the nation's new prolific thinkers. For her performance, she had projected images of herself on the Photo Booth rollercoaster filter and cut it with scenes from classic films. She had projected it against a wall in Kensington Market, and she held Miranda's hand like she was nervous. When Miranda asked Sasha what she thought the show was about, Sasha said that it was about the subversion of tradition and projection, so she could reorient what it actually means to identify as female. Afterwards, Sasha did a lot of ecstasy and skipped around town like she'd made it.

Miranda was finishing her thesis and had to have eighty thousand words submitted by December. Her work was disciplined and unrecognized. She had moved from London, Ontario, to go to Trinity College, encouraged by her father, who was a professor at Western. Her dad had finished his PhD by the time he was twenty-five and was offered three tenured positions right out of the gate. He said Trinity College was really the crème de la crème and promised he would loan Miranda money if she finished with honours. She wanted to tell him academia was different now—that the prospects for a sustainable future were bleak—but he wouldn't believe her. He'd tell her to work harder.

The doorbell of Miranda's apartment rang like a classic bell. She lived in a walk-up on the corner of Ossington and Bloor and paid fifteen hundred dollars a month and lived with an old boyfriend named Dominic.

When Miranda answered the door, it was Sasha. She leaned in and kissed Miranda in the middle of the forehead. Sasha was wearing a dress and a coat, both to the floor. Her bangs ended in a blunt line high on her forehead and she had filled in her eyebrows with a pencil crayon. Her eyeshadow was fuchsia and it made Miranda think of those girls in *Euphoria*.

"They're flying me to New York."

"Who is?"

"MoMA! They want me to do my performance. The one about food!"

Miranda smiled but her heart wasn't in it. "That's amazing," she said.

"You're coming with me! They said I could bring a companion."

"That makes me sound like a dog," Miranda said and Sasha laughed heavily, from her stomach.

They got ice cream in a cup and went to Trinity Bellwoods. Sasha fed Miranda the ice cream in small spoonfuls and talked about the show for the MoMA. Sasha was going to cover her body in weapons and also cinnamon rolls and Danish pastries. It would be a comment on food as power and danger.

Miranda understood that Sasha had disordered eating. She was always happiest when she was eating but that never lasted long. Whenever Miranda asked if she'd eaten, Sasha would get defensive and tell Miranda she had no money for food. Sasha grew up in Toronto and her mother had raised her alone. Sasha had very strong ideas about what women should be, or not be, and had known from a very young age that she would never sleep with men. Miranda, however, had slept with men for years until she got herpes and then she stopped. The first time they had sex, Miranda told Sasha she had herpes and Sasha hadn't let it bother her. She had tucked Miranda's hair behind her ear and kissed her on the nose and it made Miranda feel safe. Miranda believed she had gotten it from a guy she had known from high school named Lou, and it made her resent going home and probably made her resent men.

Sasha had convinced Miranda to go to the Blue Jays game with her that afternoon. The Jays were playing the Yankees and the game was sold out. *C Magazine* had given Sasha two tickets after she convinced them to let her write a cultural review. Miranda almost never left Parkdale and getting to the the Rogers Centre was terrible. There were a lot of people wearing blue hats and jerseys with names stitched on the back. Miranda bought a six-dollar hot dog and a fourteen-dollar beer and smoked in her seat until she was told to stop.

"Isn't this great? It's so culturally funny," Sasha said. She was leaning forward in her seat like she cared about the score. Miranda nodded and agreed that it was pretty ridiculous.

The CN Tower hung over them, casting them in a shadow, and Miranda started talking to Sasha about her research into Bill Clinton's erectile patterns. She talked about how Bill refused to cum for months.

"He must have believed that if he didn't finish that it wasn't cheating! Isn't that insane?"

"Ugh, babe, the Clintons are so over," Sasha said, taking a drag of Miranda's cigarette. "The Democrats have a serious Clinton problem, I'm telling you." Sasha was drinking a beer and a bit dribbled down her chin and Miranda kissed it off.

"Well, this isn't really about the Clintons," Miranda whispered in Sasha's ear. "It's about what makes someone presidential. And like toxic masculinity and positions of power." Sasha didn't seem to care and it made Miranda angry. "Sasha?"

"What, dude? I'm trying to listen to this fucking game. I don't even know what's going on and I have to write this thing about it."

"I'm sure you'll figure it out," Miranda said angrily and lit another cigarette even though she knew it wasn't allowed.

"What does that mean?"

"You know what it means. You're getting all this fucking attention and everyone loves your art and you're showing at the MoMA and it's all really great for you." Miranda wanted to eat her hot dog so she picked it up and it suddenly reminded her of a penis. "It would just be nice if you could listen to me for one goddamn minute. What I'm doing is important too, even if no one gives a shit."

That night, as they were about to have sex, Miranda freaked out and started pacing from wall to wall in her small room.

"What's wrong with you? You don't want to have sex, you don't want to see the Blue Jays."

Miranda lay back down beside Sasha on her red IKEA sheets and Miranda said, "I'm jealous of you."

"Why?"

"People love your stuff and it's real and weird in a way that people like, and my stuff is inaccessible and tired and my dad is paying for it."

"Your stuff is not those things," Sasha said and Miranda reached for her hand because she thought that was nice. The Penguin edition of *East of Eden* was open on Miranda's bedside table. "Why the fuck are you reading this?" Sasha asked.

"What? It's amazing."

"I read it in high school and was like so disturbed by that female character. What's her name?"

"Kate."

"Yeah. I don't know. It's like so many men have trouble writing a strong woman character without like making her evil."

Miranda thought this was probably true but also maybe too easy and she just didn't want Sasha to be right for once.

The next day, Miranda and Dominic went for lunch at Matty Matheson's new restaurant on Queen Street. Dominic reached for the bill without a conversation. He had recently been promoted to manager of Toronto's Koodo office, which was mostly a job he hated. Miranda had slept with Dominic when she was eighteen. She had just moved to the city and he was cute and normal in a way that she didn't find threatening. He had really nice blue eyes and the rest of his face was hard. He was smart in his honesty, like he wasn't trying to be difficult or critical, and he was in love with the fact that Miranda was those things as well. He was from Vancouver and he seemed constitutionally more relaxed than her, which she found people from Vancouver always were. Miranda thought this was probably because the weather was never too severe, so they didn't have to be either. Miranda used to love having sex with Dominic. He kissed her ears and ran his hands over her hips over and over again like she was a cat. When Miranda started dating women, Dominic had cried over a burger at A&W.

"It doesn't mean I'm gay, I just don't believe in limiting myself to one thing."

"I don't understand, but I'll try," he said.

Miranda understood then and many more times after that that Dominic was pretty fundamentally sexist. He mostly believed women were one thing. It didn't make her angry because she didn't think he really knew this about himself. It was just the way he had always thought about things.

"You know, I've always felt safe with Sasha," Miranda said to him over lunch. Dominic was dating a new girl named

Jen. She was blond and pretty and didn't challenge his way of thinking, which Miranda had learned was absolutely essential in his relationships. "But since she's been getting all this attention I feel like something's changed. The power dynamic or something."

Dominic drank an eighteen-dollar cocktail and nodded his head. Miranda could see he was uncomfortable with the conversation. He never knew how to talk to her about Sasha and sometimes this didn't bother her but other times she wanted to pull his hair and say, *Get over yourself.*

"You know, she's showing at the MoMA."

"Well, aren't you proud of her?"

"Yeah, I am. I'm just like jealous in this like really primal way. And I wonder if I'm feeling so competitive with her because I've like judged myself against other women my entire life. I feel like that's how women are raised—to compete with other women." Miranda stuck a scallop in her mouth and sucked on it until it began to remind her of an elbow. "You know, you see all these women in comedy and they're all just like funny and interesting and every profile of them is like, who's funnier, who's smarter, who's prettier. It's fucking crazy."

Dominic nodded his head like he was interested and Miranda loved him for that. Miranda knew she could exhaust people with her obsessive interests and her ability to talk about them until the cows came home so she had an affection for anyone who feigned interest.

Sasha's piece for *C Magazine* was insightful and funny, and she talked about how live sports allow you to return to a time of communal excitement that you become alienated from when you're older. She talked about Americanism and leisure and how baseball allowed people to return to the nostalgic past. She talked about her art practice and how most of her work was solitary but how she wanted to open herself to group projects and communal thinking. Miranda read it and ripped it out of her copy. There was a photo of Sasha in the bottom corner, and she looked impossibly cool. Her hair was cut in a triangle and she was wearing a white shirt with lots of strings. She had green eyeliner on and her bio was short and clear.

Sasha and Miranda went for drinks at a snack bar on Bathurst and Sasha talked about New York. She explained that they would leave Sunday and install the show during the week and the opening would be the following Friday.

"I don't know if I should come. I have to like write and stuff and Dominic is having this thing at our place and he wants me to be there."

"What's wrong with you?"

"Nothing is wrong with me. I just—I—"

"What?"

"Everything feels different."

"Everything *is* different because you're acting weird." Sasha often oversimplified things and it infuriated Miranda and left her feeling stupid.

Miranda ate the olive out of her martini and said, "I thought your piece in *C* was really good."

"Thank you," Sasha said. She had a tattoo of a knife near her collarbone and Miranda wanted to kiss it.

"Okay, well I'm not going to take anyone else to New York. I'd really like you to be there. I feel confused and uneven or something when you're not around."

Miranda wanted to tell Sasha that she was jealous and

that she felt insecure and scared but instead she kissed the knife.

When Miranda got home, Dominic was reading her copy of *East of Eden*. Miranda stood in the doorway and thought there was something she was attracted to in him: his curiosity, maybe.

"You look nice," he told her.

She was wearing a black dress with Stan Smiths and her hair was getting long. "Thank you." She got two beers from the fridge and handed one to Dominic as she sat down beside him on the orange couch he had inherited from Koodo headquarters.

"I like the Kate character in this book."

"You do?"

"Yeah, I think she's interesting. I feel like everyone really depends on her to make them happy but then she ruins their lives."

Miranda smiled and put her arm on the back of the sofa and leaned her cheek in her palm. Dominic was normal and uncritical, but he saw things in a way that was important. He never acknowledged the easy or the pretentious opinion. Miranda leaned in and kissed him on the lips. His facial hair scratched her chin and she thought about Sasha and how she shouldn't do this to her. Dominic kissed her cheek and then her neck and Miranda felt absolutely consumed with power.

"I have herpes."

"I know, I remember."

"I just want you to protect yourself."

"I want anything that you'll give me, Miranda."

Miranda realized then—as Dominic pulled off her dress and kissed her belly button—that he was in love with her. She wondered how long he hadn't been honest with her and she thought about Jen, the girl he was dating. She thought about Sasha and how she couldn't keep not telling her the full truth. She needed to tell her that she didn't always understand her art or think it was important. Sasha was weird but she often wasn't thoughtful and she got credit for things that were easy and uninspired. But Miranda wanted to tell her that she loved her anyway.

Dominic went down on her and afterwards Miranda told him she didn't want to have sex. "I'm sorry. I'm just confused and I don't want things to change between us." She didn't want Dominic to have all the power. It would be too predictable and that felt sad. She didn't want Dominic to keep thinking she was perfect and she didn't want to hurt Sasha and have it be made into art. She knew Sasha would have a field day portraying all the conflicting parts of Miranda's personality and she would probably get funding to do it.

Miranda went to New York with Sasha and she didn't tell her about hooking up with Dominic. The gallery flew them business class and Miranda put a hot towel on her face until it was cold. They drank wine and Sasha held Miranda's hand and thanked her for coming.

Sasha went straight to the gallery to meet the show's curator, a woman named Denver Rose, while Miranda went shopping in Soho. She bought a green sweater from Uniqlo that reminded Miranda of one she had borrowed from Sasha and ripped in the sleeve. She bought her the sweater with money her dad had loaned her for the month. Material things were all she could provide for Sasha right now, even though she knew Sasha didn't like it when Miranda bought her things just for the sake of it.

After getting lost on the Gray Line, Miranda met them at Denver's apartment in the East Village. Apparently Denver's parents had conceived her in Denver, hence the name. Miranda thought the whole thing was incredibly tacky so she went to Denver's balcony and smoked an American Spirit while looking over the river.

After leaving Denver's, Sasha convinced Miranda to go to the Empire State Building by convincing her it would be ridiculous and funny. When they got to the top, Miranda said, "I hooked up with Dominic."

The wind was blowing Sasha's hair sideways and the city looked like a postcard beneath her.

Sasha didn't respond for a while and it looked like she was occupied with everything they were standing over. "Why?" She didn't look upset and Miranda thought it was because she was too sensible to feel emotional about things she couldn't control.

"'Cause he can give you something I can't?" Sasha said.

Miranda wondered what Sasha meant but didn't ask her to clarify. "We didn't even sleep together," Miranda said. A family shoved between them for a better view of Times Square. "I just have been feeling like we're not the same anymore."

"We're not supposed to be the same just because we're women dating each other."

"I know, I just—I—" A man shoved Miranda and knocked her off balance. "I just had this idea that things would be more equal between us or something, and you're doing so well and I'm proud of you for that. But you have all the power."

"Dating men is not a great alternative if you want to feel powerful, Miranda." Sasha chuckled like she couldn't believe Miranda didn't know this.

"Dominic doesn't make me feel stupid. He doesn't make me feel like he has more important things to say. He makes it seem like everything he thinks, he thinks for the first time."

"That's a privilege that you would never give a woman though."

"I don't think that's true," Miranda said.

Sasha tucked a piece of hair behind her ear. Very lovingly, in what was almost a whisper, she told Miranda that she needed to undo what she knew about gender and power and love. She needed to find new ways to think. She made an eloquent and structured speech about how things weren't one way, and relationships were hard and complicated if you wanted them to work. She said that her art practice was a way for her to understand these things and it helped her approach new ideas in important ways. Miranda felt a lump in her throat growing, until it felt like an after-dinner mint. Sasha was making her understand things in a new way. Sasha was trying to subvert ways people thought about the most primal things: food, sex, money, power, jealousy. She wanted to change people's minds. She wanted to change her own mind. The whole moment was noisy and fleeting. There were sirens and screams and there were lights behind Sasha's head, making her glow—like an angel.

Denver Rose flew Miranda back to Toronto for free and when she got home she saw that Dominic had moved his Koodo couch out of the living room. When she asked him what was going on, he said he'd got a place closer to Lakeshore and closer to work, where people needed him if things went wrong. He told Miranda that he thought she was smart but she needed to look at her life closer than before. She told him that Sasha said that too and he laughed.

Miranda told him before he left that she liked his way of thinking and she thought it was refreshing. He acted surprised and happy that she said that.

A week later the *New York Times* profiled Sasha in their Arts section. They called her subversive and brilliant and innovative and powerful. There was a picture of Sasha eating a cinnamon roll on the front and the frosting dripped down onto her silk, collared shirt. Sasha had titled the show *Eat Me*.

SHALLOW WATER

When Gerald met Deborah, he thought about starting over. The university had sent him to Toronto to present a paper on female Canadian poets. He got money from the president's travel fund—his flight was free and so was a beer. The Sheraton was a bit expensive, but he thought, *Hey, when in Rome.* His house in Newfoundland was being renovated and he had paid a man named Al a pretty penny to redo the floors, but Al was charming and smart in a way that made Gerald believe him, so Al was redoing the roof too.

Gerald was wearing an orange bathing suit with Hawaiian print that Marilyn had bought him back in 2008 when he'd told her he was taking her somewhere tropical. Their flight had been cancelled because of the weather so they went to Jungle Jim's on Torbay Road instead. When their flight was cancelled a second and a third time, Marilyn told him to forget it.

Now, Gerald was walking through the hotel lobby in his Hawaiian bathing suit, on a baby-blue carpet that he perceived as juvenile. An Ottawa Senators towel was hanging around his neck and he thought he wouldn't see a soul. It was eleven at night and he couldn't sleep. But a woman was sitting by the shallow end of the pool. The wall behind her said SHALLOW WATER in big black letters. Her right foot was dangling in the water and he could see her toes were painted pink. She was wearing a black bathing suit, the top long enough to cover her stomach. The tile underneath her hand was pink and it matched her toes. He wondered if Marilyn painted her toenails and it made him sad that he didn't know.

"Can't sleep either?" she asked, and Gerald watched the water turn to spirals around where her right foot moved back and forth like a paddle.

"Afraid not. I have a conference in the morning and I'm nervous, but swimming usually makes me tired." Gerald reached a wet hand out to her and said, "My name's Gerald."

Her name was Deborah but she told him to call her Deb. She was a visual artist and also a waitress. She was married to a man named Rich and they had gotten in a fight about the cable bill, so she had left their house in Leslieville and walked all the way down Queen until she found a room for the night.

"You know, I always wanted a pool growing up," Deb said like it was a secret and Gerald told her he did too. He had admitted that he felt ashamed about the Sens towel and Deb told him she was short-sighted so he shouldn't worry.

He said, "You remind me of someone." It wasn't until after midnight that he realized it was his mother, who was beautiful and honest and still a mystery to him.

"So you're a poet?" Deb asked.

"No. I mean, I write poetry. But really I just study it and teach it." He thought that Marilyn would laugh if she were here now. Marilyn would remind him he hadn't written poetry in years. She would throw her head back and show her teeth. She would say that they never got what they wanted from each other.

Deb asked where his conference was and he told her it was in the lobby and that ham sandwiches were promised at noon.

"Maybe I'll come watch you speak," Deb said and he noticed her rubbing her arms with her hands.

He got out of the pool and grabbed his Senators towel. He wrapped it around her, and she said, "My husband's a Leafs fan."

Drops of water were falling down his face, making it hard for him to see. He knew that his attraction to Deb had to do with her dichotomy to Marilyn. He knew that Deb was the antithesis of everything Marilyn stood for. Marilyn knocked into everything. She disturbed things and made everything feel too full. She filled Gerald's head until there wasn't room for anything else.

The next day, Deb met him in the lobby at noon and she even had a ham sandwich. He watched her eat it and thought he had never seen someone eat finger food so beautifully. She told him that her mother used to pack her ham sandwiches every day when she was a kid. "You look sharp," she said, looking him up and down and Gerald blushed. He remembered she was short-sighted and this brought him some comfort. She was wearing a purple dress with an intentional triangle cut out of the back. Gerald thought it was kind of flashy but he appreciated her confidence. He read his paper last and talked mostly about Phyllis Webb. He talked about the CBC and how she had co-created the program *Ideas*.

"I wish I had ideas," Deb said, sipping a lemon drop martini.
"You do. I find you fascinating."

After their drink it was almost dark and Gerald realized
he'd missed two afternoon panels. Deb asked if he thought
there were leftover sandwiches so they went to the lobby and
a woman in a red jacket gave them a full sandwich cut into
quarters in a Ziploc bag.

They went to the roof of the Sheraton through the fire
escape. A man in a long-sleeved polo shirt told them that
he would prefer if they didn't go on the roof, but once he left
they did it anyway. Deb laughed with her left hand over
her mouth and the Ziploc of ham sandwiches swinging
from her right hand like a purse. Gerald thought about how
he had missed out on being rebellious. When he was younger
and everyone was doing hard drugs and having sex and
getting experienced, he'd stayed home. He always wondered
about that idea of getting experience. He was experiencing
things; they just weren't those things. He touched Deb on her
back as she climbed a small ladder to the roof and told her she
was beautiful. Deb giggled as they looked down at the city.

"Rich is probably down there," she said, and pointed to the
East End. "He's probably watching a Leafs game or something."

Gerald wished she wouldn't talk about Rich. He wanted
this experience to be his. He lay down on his back with his
hands behind his head and Deb did the same.

"I feel like I'm twenty-five again, but my hip hurts more
than it did then." Gerald had sciatica and the only relief he
could get was chewing Robaxacet until it turned to powder
in his mouth.

"I loved being twenty-five. I had so many ideas, or dreams
or something," she whispered.

Gerald had thought about the difference between his wife and Deb. He'd always thought he would be with someone like Deb when he was younger. Someone who didn't challenge him and lie to him and infuriate him. Someone who didn't throw her ideas at him like dodge balls for him to catch.

"My house is under construction."

"What does that mean?"

"It means a guy named Al is pulling the shingles off my roof." He paused and thought he saw a constellation. "And I'm married to a woman I don't understand. Or I guess I only understood her after it was too late."

Deb kissed him and for once, Gerald felt free. He wondered if this was a good thing.

Gerald spent the winter messaging Deb from a Facebook account that showed no pictures of him. In August, he asked Marilyn for a divorce. They were standing in their kitchen, which was coming down around them. Gerald told Marilyn that he was seeing a woman named Deborah and she was only in town until Friday.

"Why would you even say something?" Marilyn asked him, thinking that today was Wednesday and Friday was therefore soon. Marilyn looked around. There were men with no shirts on, wearing Levi's they had cut at the knee with her kitchen scissors. "Our house is still under construction."

"Exactly," Gerald said. "I don't always want things to be under construction."

"I don't know what you're even talking about now."

"I don't know either."

Marilyn saw Al, their carpenter, take a sledgehammer to what she was sure was a load-bearing wall.

"Al, that wall holds up the rest of the house," Marilyn yelled.

Al shrugged his shoulders with an indifference that now reminded her of her marriage. Marilyn pointed to the load-bearing wall and said, "See that, Gerald. That could be my heart!"

"What could?"

"That wall! With the hole in it!"

Gerald rolled his eyes and said, "Oh, Marilyn, stop it."

That night Gerald went to the Sheraton in St. John's to meet with Deb. She told him Rich got a deal through his work so she always stayed at the Sheraton. Her room had a view of Signal Hill and she said, "It's really cute here. Like you're in a snow globe or something."

Gerald resented it when anyone talked about the town that way but he just nodded and grabbed a mini-bottle of spiced rum from the fridge. He mixed it with Coke and it tasted awful. He looked out Deb's window and thought about his wedding and how he'd convinced Marilyn to climb Signal Hill in her wedding dress. They had never made it to the top but he remembered pulling her hand all the way down Duckworth. Her palm had felt big in his, like he was holding his own hand, and he remembered thinking they would be strong and good together, like real partners.

"I told Marilyn about you today." Deb stepped toward him and started to undo his tie. He had always seen women do this in movies and sometimes when he watched porn, although that was almost never. It always felt wrong. "I can just take the tie off myself," he said as he started to sweat.

"What's wrong, Gerald?" Deb sat down on the king-sized

bed and looked up at him. The fitted sheet on the top right corner sprung off the mattress and there was a tiny stain there that made Gerald shiver. He put his hand over his mouth so she couldn't hear his answer. He ran to the bathroom and knocked a miniature shampoo and conditioner from the side of the bath as he fell on his knees and vomited into the toilet, tasting the spiced rum in his throat. He crossed his arms on the toilet seat and for a second he thought about praying even though he hadn't gone to church since he was a kid. He rinsed his mouth and walked back to the room. Deb was under the sheets on the bed. *This is what you've always wanted*, Gerald reminded himself.

He climbed under the sheets and said, "I just threw up."

"Oh, that's okay," Deb said and stroked his head like he was a child. Like he would do better next time.

Deb was confusing in bed. She made sounds that Gerald thought happened at the wrong moments. She moved a lot and changed positions and he couldn't hold onto her. She kept asking him what he wanted and he thought about Marilyn and how she made things hard for him, especially when they had sex. She was substantial and difficult. With Deb, he didn't know what to do with his hands. He felt distracted and confused by being able to please her so easily and by being able to give her what she wanted. He rolled off her and realized that all the corners of the fitted sheet had now come off the mattress, in toward their bodies like a trap.

Marilyn had been lying on her back since Wednesday. Gerald would check in on her every afternoon when he got home from the gym, and say, "This isn't normal, Marilyn!"

Marilyn didn't respond when Gerald said this because

she blamed the dissolution of her marriage on her desire for the normal things almost as much as she blamed him. She wondered if Gerald had taken Deborah to the airport on Friday and if he'd kissed her on the mouth outside Tim Hortons. She wondered if they kissed with tongue. And if he got a honey cruller on the way out—his favourite. Marilyn never let him eat honey crullers, which she cursed herself for now. He hadn't slept in the bed since he had told her about Deborah. She wondered where he was sleeping, since their couch was wrapped in plastic, the thick kind that protects things from getting damaged.

Sometimes the dog, Anne (named after Anne Carson) would lie beside her under the covers, on its back. *This dog is my real partner*, she would think. Then she would yell, "You hear that, Gerald! The dog is my real partner!" Anne wouldn't move for such long periods that Marilyn would have to put her hand on the dog's heart just to make sure it wasn't dead. She wondered if Gerald ever thought about putting his hand on her heart.

Gerald was an English professor at the university. He had grown up in Mount Pearl and done all his degrees at Memorial. Marilyn knew he always felt best when he knew everything about something and that he never wanted to leave Newfoundland. He left the house every morning at seven and went to the gym on campus every evening at five. Marilyn wondered if he'd met Deborah at school. She couldn't ask, though, because that would require getting up and acknowledging that things weren't normal.

Since Monday, Marilyn had spent a considerable amount of time staring at the ceiling, thinking about ways to avoid seeing her husband ever again. But now, with fear, she yelled

Gerald's name like she needed him. Instead of Gerald, Al rushed into the bedroom.

"There's a wet spot spreading across the ceiling!"

"Yes, well, I had to redo the roof. The water's gettin' in 'cause the foundation's weak."

"No shit." Marilyn started shaking. There was something so fundamentally threatening about the roof coming down. The wet patch was spreading across the ceiling and she suddenly felt vulnerable and she hated that it was Al who was here to see it. She should have been more vulnerable for Gerald. She should have tried harder to be what he needed her to be.

Al wrapped his arms around Marilyn and told her to breathe. She wanted to push him off and accuse him of dismantling her home.

"Do you like your job? Renovating?" Marilyn asked.

"Nice being able to change what people are unhappy with."

When people asked how she and Gerald met, Marilyn always said, with the ease of someone who lied often, "Oh, we met in college." When this happened, Gerald never dared to correct her but she always knew he wanted to. They'd actually met online, something Marilyn would never admit. It was the same when people asked if they had kids. Marilyn would say, "One day," but she knew Gerald liked her better when she told the truth. But most things about Marilyn were not honest. She wanted two kids with blond hair and probably freckles too. And her body wouldn't let her have that, so she lied. She constructed stories that would allow people to believe those things were coming. And everyone was nice and they would take a sip of their wine and say, "I'm excited for you, Marilyn."

Marilyn felt now as if she and Gerald had made a deal years ago to use each other to get what they wanted out of the rest of their lives. She realized somewhere along the way that she married Gerald so she could show people her life had really started. It was like they'd connected their pinkies and promised to help each other get by in the way people were supposed to.

Marilyn was living at her mother's house in Ottawa and decided to visit Gerald in Newfoundland after she was laid off from her public relations job at Parliament. She had just turned thirty-five when she'd met Gerald on Plenty of Fish. She had made a mistake with her settings and didn't specify how far away a desired partner would live. So after five phone calls on her mother's landline, Marilyn visited St. John's and Gerald picked her up from the airport. He had a receding hairline that was more severe than in his picture and he was eating a honey cruller.

She moved in with Gerald right away, which felt terribly wrong but she was committed to being more risky and living her life on the edge. Newfoundland made her feel on the edge of something, she just didn't know what. When Gerald went to work during the day, Marilyn would go to the Good Life on Water Street, where they promised her a better body, fast.

Marilyn and Gerald spent the first three months tiptoeing around each other. Marilyn realized that he liked late-night snacks and he hated when anyone's toothbrush touched his. The sparse hairs on his chest were like little islands and they made Marilyn think of Newfoundland. Marilyn told Gerald that when she was younger everyone told her she could do anything she wanted, so she had never narrowed her thinking. This made her constantly unsure of what she was really passionate about.

Marilyn liked being in Gerald's house. She spread her stuff around so he wouldn't ever forget she was there. She put her toothbrush in the holder beside his, close but not touching. One night, over a rotisserie chicken Gerald had picked up after work, he asked her to marry him. They had a balcony that faced the Narrows and the sky was a cotton-candy pink. She had smiled and put her hand on his shoulder, which felt bigger since he had started working out. He opened a bottle of red wine that had been on sale and it tasted too sour for the moment but they pretended it was great. Marilyn's face got pink when she drank the wine, and Gerald told her she matched the sky.

When Gerald got home and saw the leaky roof, he swore, and then he convinced Marilyn to take a room at the Holiday Inn. He drove them to Portugal Cove Road in the blue Ford Escape that he'd purchased after tenure. Marilyn remembered when he got tenure. She bought two party hats and she wore hers tilted to the left, the string sinking into her chin and holding it in place. She had kissed him on the cheek and told him she was proud that he got what he always wanted, security.

"Are you hungry? They have an East Side Mario's! Bottomless soup and bread is what I hear," he said as they passed the Sheraton.

Marilyn was staring out the window and thinking about their wedding. Gerald had bought her a corsage like for a high school prom and it flew around on her wrist, orange petals flying into the northeast winds as they climbed Signal Hill. Gerald thought it would be romantic to get to the top, but Marilyn said, halfway up, "Gerald, I need my puffer."

So there she was, thirty-six and already grey by the ears, sucking on a puffer in her wedding dress from the Avalon Mall Sears. Gerald took a photo of her with a disposable camera that they got developed two Septembers later. Marilyn's hair was all over the place, her veil almost horizontal in the wind.

"Well, that's a sight for sore eyes. Did we even make it to the top? I don't remember," Marilyn said when they got the photos back.

"No, we never made it to the top, Marilyn."

East Side Mario's was themed like New York City and Marilyn said, "I hate it when they do this. Try to convince me that I'm not on an island in the middle of nowhere but actually in the middle of Times Square. Why do people even like this?"

"I think they find it exciting," Gerald said. "Not everyone can afford a vacation." He thought of Hawaii and the trip they'd never taken.

After eating cheese cappelletti and four bowls of Italian wedding soup, Marilyn said, "You know, I was just thinking about our wedding."

Gerald swallowed and said, "I'm sorry about all this." Again, Marilyn wondered if he meant the roof or their marriage.

"You know what I did today? I looked up *renovation* on thesaurus.com."

Gerald stared into his soup bowl like it was a mirror.

"You know what the results were, Gerald? Improvement. Renewal. Upgrade."

"Marilyn, I'm sorry."

"You know what the antonyms were?"

"I don't want to know."

Marilyn rolled up the sleeve of her cardigan and said, "Look, I wrote them on my arm so I wouldn't forget."

Across her big, pale arm, it said DAMAGE, DESTRUC-TION, HARM, HURT, INJURY, NEGLECT, in Marilyn's bold writing. She had the handwriting of a confident person.

Gerald ate a piece of garlic bread and the crumbs fell on his dress shirt and stayed there. This was the side of his wife he didn't understand, the challenging and dramatic side of her that was so opposite of who he believed he was. "I didn't mean to hurt you, or damage you, or neglect you. I wouldn't have, if it didn't feel good, with Deb."

The short form of his lover's name left his mouth and hit her like a high school spitball. Marilyn tilted her head to the side like she did in pictures and began to understand that Gerald was with this woman because it was easier than being with her. She wanted to tell him to grow up and realize that most things were never easy and that he had made commitments and attachments.

"I feel so far from you," Marilyn said instead. "Like I'm in New York City."

Gerald only got one room, with two twin beds, and told her it was a hell of a lot cheaper. Marilyn got Cheezies from the vending machine and her mouth quickly turned orange. They took the elevator up to the second floor and she could see all angles of her and Gerald in the mirrored walls of the elevator.

When they got to the room, Marilyn said, "We have a room facing the pool."

Gerald thought about the night he met Deb and it made him feel dirty now. Like he was hiding the truth from Marilyn, even though she hid the truth from him all the time. The bedspreads were pink and floral. Gerald's mother had told him to never sit on a bed without turning the bedspread down.

Marilyn fell back on the bedspread with her hands open like a star. "It's nice to stare at a new ceiling."

"See, this is kind of like a holiday."

"You can't say that because the hotel says *holiday* in the name." Marilyn turned on her side and her dark hair fell behind her. "We never took a proper holiday, Gerald."

"You called it off, remember?"

"No. That's not how I remember it." Marilyn got up and grabbed a white hand towel from the chair. "I'm going for a swim."

Gerald turned down the bedspread and sat down with his book. It was short stories by Mary Gaitskill, *Bad Behavior*. He used to hate Gaitskill but she was Deb's favourite author. She told him over Facebook that there was something liberating about Gaitskill and that it was seductive. She couldn't believe it didn't seduce him. Gerald told Deb that he liked rules and structure and poetry. He told her he always played it safe. And it felt good to not follow the rules with her, like his whole body was on fire. Or like he was playing with fire. He told her he stopped reading male authors in 2010 because he wanted help understanding his wife. Now, he sat with *Bad Behavior*. He felt guilty; it felt like a stomach ache. He thought this was maybe what he had always been trying to avoid while he was growing up. Feeling guilty about doing the wrong thing. Lying felt like a burden he couldn't bear. Like it would disrupt the foundation.

He got up and looked through the window and over the pool. Marilyn was in a floral one-piece bathing suit, doing the butterfly. Marilyn's body was never what she wanted it to be. She had asthma and a birthmark on her neck. She had big shoulders and an inhospitable uterus. She looked elegant to him now, though. She would throw her arms in circles and her back would arch before she was underwater and blurry again. He watched her hoist her body out of the water and grab her towel. She leaned against the metal pole that was there to hold people steady and stuck her right foot in the water. There was lettering stretching across the wall behind her that said SHALLOW WATER. He leaned forward until his breath fogged on the bedroom window. He could have sworn that his wife was crying. His chest felt tight and he thought, *It's okay, it's probably just water from the pool*, and then he saw her big shoulders shake. He wanted to be home with her, holding her under the leaky roof. He wanted her to lie to him and say she was okay so things could just keep being normal. He wanted to never tell her that when Deb visited Newfoundland last week she had told him she was getting sick in the mornings.

He looked back at his book, open at the spine. He realized he didn't want this, this bad behaviour, the spontaneity of not knowing what was next. He wanted to feel the boredom of the life he had built with Marilyn. He wanted to be ordinary and he didn't know why he'd been mad at Marilyn for wanting that too and giving it to him.

The lights were off when Marilyn returned to the room. She went to the bathroom and left the door open. When she stepped out, Gerald was lying on his back with his eyes closed.

"I miss Anne Carson," he said.

"Mmmm, me too," Marilyn replied as she got into her

own bed. She lay the same way as Gerald and said, "Did you notice she's losing her hair?"

"She's stressed."

The room fell silent and they could only hear the fan from the bathroom. "I forgot to turn it off."

"I'll get it," Gerald said as the bedsprings screamed underneath him. He was wearing blue checkered boxers that Marilyn could make out in the dark. She'd bought them with their Costco membership for his fiftieth birthday. Gerald stubbed his toe and swore under his breath.

"This all feels normal," he said as he returned to bed and it made Marilyn smile.

When he was lying on his back, the way he was before, and Marilyn could hear his breathing turn steady, she said, "The words on my arm, they washed off in the water."

SUGAR

My blood sugar was so high that winter that my doctor told me I really had to watch it. I told him I was buying a lot of those little bags of candy that you could get at Needs or Halliday's right by the front counter. I tried to convince him they were hard to avoid buying and he said I needed to try harder.

The night after my doctor's appointment, my boyfriend and I watched *The Shining* in my bed. I had rearranged my room the week before and everything still felt out of order.

"Do you think it's better this way?"

"I don't know, I feel like we had a lot of nice memories when your room was organized the other way and now those memories feel like further away or something."

Jacob said this as he finished a handful of Spicy Nacho Doritos. I kept looking at his hand every time it would leave the bag, waiting for him to wipe nacho dust onto my striped IKEA bedspread, which I'd ordered the month before.

"I think that's crazy. The memories just happened over there on that wall instead of this one." I pointed my finger straight out to the opposing wall and Jacob grabbed my finger and rolled on top of me. He kissed me and his breath tasted like nachos.

"Dude, Danny is riding that toy car on the big carpets, you love this part!"

Jacob kissed my cheek and rolled off me. "You're right. This part is the best."

We watched the rest of the movie in the dark and I could hear my roommates in the kitchen padding around in a way that made my heart feel full. My roommate Helen had started baking specialty cakes for people in St. John's and she was blowing up. People were hiring her to make their wedding cakes and their birthday cakes and cakes for office parties and retirement parties. Helen had started ordering piping tips of different sizes and designs on Amazon and they would come in really tiny packages in the mail every week and every time one arrived it would make her happy.

There was a knock on my bedroom door and it was Helen. "Do you guys want a slice of cake?" she yelled through the door.

"Come in!"

Helen opened the door and on a tiny plate rimmed with flowers there was a slice of a cake with pink icing that she was making for a christening that weekend.

"They cancelled the christening," Helen said. "I guess they changed their mind and they don't want to baptize the baby? I don't know, Christianity seems crazy to me." She had icing on her cheek and her hair was tied in a bun on top of her head.

"You look nice," I told her and Jacob nodded his head and hummed while he picked up the cake and took a bite. There was something so unselfconscious about Helen when she was working that I thought suited her. It was one of the only times that she wasn't in her head and overthinking everything.

"How was *The Shining*?"

"It was good," Jacob said. Jacob was taking an advanced film seminar at MUN about the cinematography of Stanley Kubrick and he was making me watch all of Kubrick's hits. Last week had been *Eyes Wide Shut*, next week *2001*.

"I don't know, dude," I interrupted. "Kubrick seems crazy, like don't you think this movie is just supposed to be a warning against the American nuclear family or whatever? And how like you're going to die probably if you try to imitate that tradition 'cause it's ultimately just like bullshit?"

Jacob took another bite of the cake and offered me the plate. I reminded him that my doctor told me I had to watch my sugar consumption and so he finished the slice.

"I think you're creating a narrative that's not there about all this nuclear family stuff," he said with his mouth full.

Helen had left the room and I could hear her humming in the kitchen.

"Well, if it's not a warning against that, it's sure as hell a warning against men who have creative ambitions or like any sort of power in the family structure. Don't you think?"

Jacob laughed and said, "All work and no play makes Jacob a dull boy," and then he kissed me and his mouth tasted like cake.

A week later, a girl I used to work with at the Keg when I was sixteen, Carla, started advertising on her Facebook page that she was sugaring out of her house in Paradise. Sugaring was this new way of waxing that everyone was talking about. I called her on a phone number I had saved for ages and told her I wanted to book an appointment for a Brazilian. Jacob thought I was being ridiculous but I told him I wanted to see what all the fuss was about. I took the bus up Kenmount Road all the way and then walked the rest.

Carla answered the door and she looked the exact same except she had a deep wrinkle in the middle of her forehead and a vertical wrinkle between her eyes. She hugged me and it felt nice. She told me to go into her bathroom and change and wipe between my legs with one of the facecloths she had stacked on the counter that were all different colours. She stepped behind a white curtain and waited for me to let her know when I was lying on the bed she had set up in her living room. The TV was on beside me, playing CNN. Donald Trump had shut down the government and wouldn't reopen it until he had his wall built at the border. I felt relaxed by CNN. Like it was just noise that didn't make any sense and trying to make sense of it was pointless. Carla stuck her hand into a vat of a substance that was essentially honey and used this ball of honey to remove all the hair from around my vagina. She kept on telling me I was doing well, as if I was accomplishing something big.

"So what are you even up to these days?"

I took a long breath through my nose and held the skin on my stomach, waiting for the next rip of hair. "Um, I'm working on a manuscript for my master's degree," I said, finishing the sentence quickly so I could prepare for the pain.

"Oh yeah, what are you writing about?"

"Um, I guess just like some modern short stories about like technology and Instagram and feeling empty and shit like that." Trying to articulate what I was doing seemed so sad in that moment.

Carla ripped the hair out of my flesh. "You're doing really well," she said again.

"Thank you," I replied and I felt a tear leak out of my left eye and down the side of my face.

After it was done, my crotch felt sticky and sore. I went back to Carla's bathroom and changed back into the Levi's I had bought at Value Village the week before. Carla was on the other side of the curtain. She thanked me for supporting her new business endeavour and I thanked her for supporting me too. She gave me purple exfoliating gloves that I put in my pocket and I told her I would fulfill her aftercare regimen. She hugged me again and wished me good luck with my book. I gave her the fifty-dollar bill my father had gifted me for Christmas, and a tip, and I started walking through Paradise to the bus stop. Walking felt weird and my pants were irritating my crotch where it had been sugared. I climbed a snowbank outside Carla's house to avoid a patch of ice and fell anyway. When I got up and started walking again, I was crying uncontrollably in a way that felt so involuntary it felt almost like a betrayal. It had started getting dark at four p.m. in St. John's and this year—more than ever—I found it depressing and heavy. I missed the sun and I missed feeling okay.

I called Jacob and he answered on the third ring.

"What are you doing?" I said between sobs.

"I'm watching *Eyes Wide Shut* again. Do you think it's all supposed to be a dream?"

"I don't know . . . uh maybe."

"Hey, what's wrong?"

"I don't know, I feel so sad. I just feel like I always thought I was doing this really important work with my writing and

I thought I had this big and sparkly future with it and I just feel like I haven't even done anything since I stopped working at the Keg with this girl when I was sixteen and I just feel like all these things I thought about myself are just like things I tell myself so I can feel okay but they're not actually based on any kind of truth." I finished speaking and could see my breath in front of my face like fog. "And it's so fucking cold out and now I don't have any pubic hair."

"Do you want me to come get you? My mom said I can borrow the Jetta while they're in Florida."

"Okay. I'm going to walk to Chapters and maybe you'll pick me up there?"

"Okay. Don't freak out too much. You scare me when you're insecure."

When Jacob and I got home, all the lights were off and Helen had left cupcakes on the table with a pink Post-it attached that said *Eat Me!* So I sat down on the counter and ate six.

"I think you're just feeling all these assurances around you dissolving," Jacob said. He was sitting on the floor with his back against the counter. "And it's not one thing in particular. But then you start to feel like all these things you're attached to will fulfill your desires for this like full life when in fact they probably won't."

"Isn't that so depressing though, like why do we attach ourselves to things if they don't make our lives better?"

"I don't know. I don't know anything."

By the time Helen got home, all the cupcakes were gone and even though I felt empty, I felt full.

MY FRIEND, MY PARROT

The week Princess Diana died, my brother, Neil, got a parrot. I remember this because my mother was a wreck. I think they call them a flashbulb memories: you can remember exactly where you were and what you were doing when something significant happened. My mother claims she can still smell the polish from the manicure she was getting when JFK was shot. But it was different with Diana. My mother cut all her hair and dyed it blond, and at one point I really thought that a tiara was right around the corner. My brother, six at the time and too young to appreciate my mother's sadness, begged for a parrot. And my mother didn't have the strength to fight him. She hadn't slept in days. My brother trained the parrot to repeat everything. One day he got in a fight with my mother as she looked at a Princess Diana coffee-table book.

"I want to watch TV!" Neil yelled.

"I want to watch TV!" the parrot yelled.

"Well, that's too bad. They're televising the funeral today," my mother said. She had strategically placed Kleenex beside her and she had worn black for the occasion. Her feet were crossed beside a martini on the coffee table.

"You didn't even know this person! She's dead!"

My mother looked up at Neil, and from where I was sitting in the kitchen I could see her eyes looked watery.

"She's dead!" the parrot yelled from his cage in the corner of the room.

My mother started crying.

"She's dead!" the parrot said again. "She's dead!"

I think my brother started to feel bad around then. He took the parrot out of its cage and put it on his shoulder. He went to his bedroom and shut the door, but the parrot wouldn't stop reminding us of death.

My best friend's parents are rich. They live in a gated community in Guelph called Rolling Hills and their house is white and long with triangular windows and a baby grand piano in the middle of the living room like a rug. My best friend's name is Diana and she reminds me of a princess. Her parents sat her down last week and told her they were seeing other people but they would stay in the house and nothing would change. They didn't want to split their assets. Diana's room had a door off the side that was practically an invitation for her to start smoking. She bought long, thin cigarettes and she looked elegant and beautiful when she smoked. She had short blond hair that a boy had cut on an angle at a party the previous week.

"Men don't like to be contradicted," she told me as I complained about how I got a different kind of attention than her.

"That's insane," I told her. She shrugged like she had long ago accepted this fact as truth, and her life was structured around it.

Diana wanted to be a writer. She had told me this on her

back stoop, as she smoked a cigarette and I ate all-dressed chips with her Hudson's Bay blanket wrapped around my shoulders.

"I just have so many stories to tell."

"Yeah. I don't really know if that matters to me as much," I said. I had started writing a lot the year before, when we had entered high school. I knew how to craft a strong sentence and my English teacher was looking to find me scholarship opportunities. But I just didn't have the same experiences Diana did. And I wondered if this would matter. For a long time, I thought Diana was a liar. She told stories that always seemed fictional. She had done mushrooms with her parents' gardener or slept with her chemistry professor in his wife's Kia Soul. But over time I realized that she wasn't a liar, she was just different than I was. Things were easier for her. She could climb hills without breathing heavily and she knew how to put her hand on a boy's arm. She was like a rare bird. A parrot, maybe.

I was really close to my brother. I was three years older than him and all the things he did reminded me of me. We used to lie in his bed and entwine our feet. On Fridays when we were younger we always rented a movie at the Blockbuster next to the grocery store and we bought snacks with our allowance. After he got the parrot, though, we stopped watching movies and I started spending more time at our father's house down the street. Our father's girlfriend, Anne, had recently moved in and she was pretty. And the house smelled like flowers, which I decided I liked. When I asked Anne if she liked Princess Diana she shrugged her shoulders like she wasn't too attached. I liked this about her. She didn't get too emotional about things. She just let them slide off her back like water. I would braid her hair and I would think about my mother and how nothing was easy for her. I think my father was happier with Anne because she could let things go, she could let them slide. She didn't ask too much of him.

Whenever I went over to my dad's, Anne would say, "How are things shakin', Bri?"

I wanted her to stop repeating herself. It made me think about the parrot which Neil had recently named Charles. The name was a cruel reminder for my mother of the royal family. My mom was inclined to attach herself to things that had no actual bearing on her real life; she was actually protecting herself.

"How's your mother?"

"She's fine. She's still upset about Princess Diana." My father rolled his eyes as he cut cheese into cubes at the counter. "I don't know," I said. "I think she really loved her. She thought she was so beautiful."

"I wish your mother could learn to have a regular reaction to things," my father said as he violently threw the knife into the sink beside him. "And I don't even know why she bought you guys that fucking parrot." My father's neck was turning red like a rash and Anne rubbed her hand on his back in clockwise circles.

"Well, I mean, it's like we have another sibling in the house, which can be frustrating. But Neil is really happy and I think it's teaching him about attachment and maturity. You know, he's never had to watch out for anything else. I've watched over him, and Mom has watched over me, and so now it's his turn."

My father was looking at me while he leaned against the

kitchen counter. He looked upset that I hadn't included him in my breakdown of who took care of whom, but he didn't say I was wrong. He just turned around.

"You know, parrots are actually really beautiful and you should see this one. It's yellow but in a way that almost looks like blond hair." I pointed at Anne. "Like yours, kinda." Anne smiled. "And parrots are basically almost extinct so it's special and rare and it's important for Neil to be around Charles, he's intelligent and entertaining and—"

"Who the hell is Charles?" my father asked.

"Charles is the parrot, Dad." I didn't know why I was defending Charles when it wasn't very long ago I was resenting the bird's relationship with Neil. But it felt important to acknowledge that there was a new man in our house where my father used to be.

A boy named Aaron Walker asked me to go to the moving carnival at Stone Road Mall on the weekend. He picked me up from my mother's house and kissed her on the cheek, which I thought was nice. It had been a while since the parrot had died but we all still paused, waiting for it to speak. When we got to the mall, Aaron parked at the back of the parking lot so we could look at the carnival.

"The rides can all be dismantled in like a night and then they just move to the next town and set up in their parking lot," Aaron said, like I hadn't been coming to this carnival every year since I was a kid.

"I want things to be more complicated than that." I turned toward him so my knee was shoved against the gearshift. "You know, when I was younger, my brother had a parrot."

"That's sick. Did it like talk and stuff?"

"Yeah. It was like this living, breathing thing in our house, with a voice. My brother basically stopped talking after he got it."

"That's so weird, dude."

"Yeah. And this one year, my mom wanted to take us to this carnival so we could ride the apples." I pointed to the ones I was talking about. "And my brother wouldn't leave the house without the parrot. So my brother brought the parrot to the carnival and it rode the apples with us."

Aaron laughed and then leaned over the gearshift and kissed me.

"You're interesting," he said.

I didn't respond because I didn't want to be interesting. I wanted to be something else. But I liked him too. We rode the apples and I puked on his shoes afterwards. Then we got cotton candy and I ate it in the front seat as Aaron drove me home.

As we pulled into my driveway he brought up the parrot again. "What happened to it?"

"It died." I turned and looked at Aaron and ran my hands through his hair because I thought it would be nice. "My brother was never the same. The parrot took his voice."

When Charles died, we buried him in the backyard under the tree with my brother's tree house. Neil cried until he had the hiccups and my mother wore the same dress she wore when they buried Princess Diana. I recognized the embroidered collar and was happy for a second that my mother never threw anything out.

"He was the best friend a boy could have," Neil said while he placed a dandelion the same colour as Charles on his grave.

"I think he brought honesty back to this house after Dad left," I said and my mother cried at this and dabbed at her cheeks with her sleeve. "He was intelligent and important and I'll miss him."

Afterwards, the three of us had pigs in a blanket that my mother had heated up in the oven but that were still cold on the inside.

"Do you think I'll ever have another friend like him?" my brother asked.

The house seemed so quiet it was almost eerie. I didn't know what to say and I didn't know how to fill the silence. That was Charles's job.

"I think you'll find someone better than Charles," I told Neil and he looked at me like I'd slapped him. "I just, I think that you'll find someone who has new and interesting things to say, things that will help you think and learn."

"I don't know if I want that," Neil said and I thought maybe I didn't either. It was nice to just have Charles say back to you what you said to him. It made it feel important, like it was worth repeating. Maybe we were all just looking to have our ideas reaffirmed. We were looking for validation, we were looking to be flattered and copied. I wondered if this was why my parents had called it quits. My mother was never interested in copying anyone. She was unique and obsessive and she hardly ever gave people what they wanted.

I didn't meet anyone who could imitate the human voice like Charles until I met Diana. I would tell a joke and a week later I would hear her tell the same one. I would write a story and she would write one in the same voice. I had broken things off with Aaron because I was scared to talk to him. He thought

I didn't know how to communicate and I told him he was probably right. I wondered why, so I went to see the high school guidance counsellor. Her office was an off-white and the couch inside was green.

"My brother and I used to be really close, but then Charles, his parrot, just gave him things that I couldn't."

The guidance counsellor kept crossing her legs and uncrossing them and it made me angry that she couldn't make a decision.

"I think your father leaving so quickly must have been very difficult for you."

"No, it felt fine," I said. I ate a sour candy from a dish on the guidance counsellor's desk. It was yellow and I thought that meant lemon but it was really banana, which I didn't like. I left and didn't feel any different. I think I just wanted the guidance counsellor to agree with me and tell me that I was right and that it was in fact the parrot that fucked me up by giving me a false sense of confidence and by never challenging me.

Diana and I went to the Salvation Army in her mom's Lexus and tried to find treasure. I was flipping through the men's jeans when Diana said, "I kissed Aaron." She looked up at me for affirmation. "He told me he thinks I'm interesting."

I didn't say anything and moved to look at dishes. I was willing her not to follow me. I was always the best at finding things while thrifting, but Diana looked hotter than I did. She found short shirts in the kids' section, tiny crop tops she would cut the sleeves off. I picked up a skirt with flowers on it and put it in my cart but when I got to the change room it didn't fit right.

Diana tried it on after me and said, "I'm buying it."

"No you're not," I said from the change room next to hers.

"What's wrong with you?"

"You don't just get to take the things I don't want. You can't just take my ideas and my boyfriend and make it yours."

"I don't do that."

It was strange doing this while I wasn't looking at her. It made it easier to have this divide between us, something that could separate us enough so that I could finally be honest. "Yes you do!" I said. "You change it just enough so that you think I won't notice. And part of me thinks you won't notice! And then you can continue pretending you're morally better than I am."

I could tell Diana left the change room because I could hear the door slam and I couldn't see her feet anymore. I opened my change room too and she was standing there, holding a discount sweater that reminded me of my mother. Diana didn't even need to shop at the thrift store, since her dad would buy her anything she wanted online. I wanted to pretend this had nothing to do with her extreme wealth but I knew that didn't help.

"You're the one who pretends you're morally superior. You judge me for drinking too much and having sex with people. You pretend you're above all that and you get mad at me for not living the same way you do!"

"That's not true," I said and suddenly I felt hot, like she had found me out. "You steal things from me."

"Only because you want me to."

Diana walked away and I watched her throw the skirt I had picked out—the one with the flowers—onto a rack with the loafers, like she didn't want it anymore. I called a cab to take me home and I left everything I had found behind too.

I stood outside waiting for the cab and I felt cold but also hot. My chest was tight and I felt bad for all the things I didn't say. I wanted to tell Diana that I thought she was beautiful like a princess and that her hair was the same colour as my brother's dead parrot. I wanted to tell her that I would never find anyone else like her and that parrots were becoming extinct. It was becoming harder and harder to find them. I wanted to tell her that it was true, I judged her when she did things I wouldn't do and got mad when she did things I would. I wanted to tell her that we buried my brother's parrot in the ground and put a dandelion on top of him. I wanted to tell her that I hoped she would never die. I started crying and I dabbed my cheeks with my sleeve, like my mother. I hopped in the back of the cab and the man asked my address. I gave him Diana's address in Rolling Hills and I crossed my legs underneath me.

"You okay, sweetie?" the cab driver asked and it made me feel taken care of.

I nodded and hoped he would understand me. As we were driving down the Hanlon in silence I noticed he had a toy parrot hanging from his rear view mirror. It was green and yellow and I thought it was beautiful.

"Do you have a parrot?" I asked.

"I used to. Best friend I ever had."

IKEA SHOWROOM

tell them them start at step one. Stay organized! Stay positive! It's all easier than it looks! Ha. The caller sometimes laughs but mostly cries, and I tell them they're good and worthy of things that fit together. I tell them this is what we want. We need to know how we can improve and be there for you in the way you need us to be. I tell people to follow instructions to build things that will never fall apart. Unless you wear them down of course! I usually laugh after I say that. Some people say they don't want my help, and a lot of women say they always feel men are trying to break things down for them in ways they don't want. When they say this, I usually transfer them to Jenna.

Our cubicles are separated by dividers that vary in their primary colours. They are translucent enough for me to see Jenna's silhouette. How she crosses her legs when she needs to pee and puts her hair in a ponytail when she's bored. The dividers don't let me see her face, though. I hear her say to a customer, "It's okay, stay positive," and I think, *God, she's good.*

People usually call before they've exhausted all their options. They say, "I don't speak Swedish," and I say, "The trick is the pictures. If you look at the full picture, you'll be able to see where you're going wrong." They usually grunt here. A lot of people tell me that nothing fits where it's supposed to, or it doesn't make sense.

"Everything that's worth anything is complicated though, right!?"

A lot of people say, "No, I only want the simple things."

I usually look at Jenna when they say this, but I can't actually see her.

The company sends its employees to the store in Brooklyn at the end of every year and encourages us to explore how things work. The company says: A new year is coming up, and people want to put things together. I stick my head over the divider and ask Jenna if she wants a ride to Brooklyn.

She is eating a salad with a vinegar dressing and her legs are crossed. She says, "I can only see your eyes and not your mouth, only a little bit of your nose."

"It's weird to look at someone talk without seeing their mouth move. Where's all the noise coming from, you know? It's like the neighbour in Home Improvement."

Our floor of the building is called *Home Improvement*. Jenna says yes to a ride.

When I pick her up, I am wearing my blue and yellow striped uniform shirt. Jenna is wearing a white T-shirt and jeans and I say, "Where's your uniform?"

She explains that corporate encouraged them to dress regularly. "We don't want people to think we know how to assemble everything."

"But then we would be tricking them. It would be dishonest."

"Customers don't want to feel like there's something they can't do that we can. This way we all share the struggle of trying to build something."

I nod my head. "I guess you're right." I drive us from Jersey to the Brooklyn store at 1 Beard Street. I tell Jenna to look out at the water.

"It's the Statue of Liberty," Jenna says.

"Who do you think built it?"

Jenna laughs. "I wonder if there were steps."

When we enter the store Jenna and I get meatballs and cornbread and Jenna moans while she eats. She sucks chocolate milk out of a small straw and calls it delish. We walk downstairs and through rooms that lead to rooms I didn't know were there. Jenna tells me to wait up. We are supposed to record our findings on clipboards the front desk gave us. Mini-pencils swing from the clipboards like bungee jumpers and Jenna and I hold our clipboards upside down, laughing at our complete control of the movement.

"I know how to build everything here," Jenna says as we step into a children's room.

I say, "I know, me too. I think it's the only time I've ever felt useful."

Jenna sits down on the bed and I think of her holding a baby. The baby sucking her breast. Latched onto her like a secret.

"Come on, we have to rate the furniture in here." She bends down to check out the bed frame assembly and I think of her picking up a soother.

"How do you think everything looks?" she asks.

"Perfect," I say before entering the room.

We stop in the primary bedroom next and Jenna lies down against the pillows on the double bed and pats the spot beside her twice. She puts down her clipboard and connects her hands behind her head. I lie down beside her and wish I wasn't wearing my uniform shirt. I connect my hands the same way as hers and stare at the ceiling. It's the top floor of the building and there's a big wet patch on the ceiling above us. A drop of water drips onto Jenna's face and I think it's a tear. I wipe it with my thumb and she connects our hands against the bedspread.

"We should tell someone about the ceiling," Jenna says as we continue to stare at it. "Everything from this room should probably be moved out."

"Should we offer to take the furniture apart for them? People are never good at dismantling."

After we fill out our clipboards with our tiny pencils we tell the front desk there's a leak in Primary Bedroom Showroom 4 and offer our services. "We're from Home Improvement."

"We'll take care of it," they say, and I think, *We'll see.*

I kiss Jenna in Bathroom Showroom 6. I know the mirror beside us was assembled in nine steps. I watch the men down the hallway take apart the double bed we were just lying on and I kick the bathroom door shut.

Jenna says, "Should we get in the shower?"

SOFT SERVE

Hugh

I told Janice to meet me on Deck Eleven, where the soft serve was sweeter than Deck Six. The ship was docked in St. Lucia and everyone else was on land. With no one by the pool, the deck looked like a David Hockney painting. There were lawn chairs running along the perimeter of the top floor. The lawn chairs were the classic kind with the bands and the holes in between, big enough for an arm to sink into, or a leg. The cruise director encouraged everyone to leave the ship on days at port but I was always too lazy and I wasn't good at following instructions. My parents and grandparents got off the ship that morning with sunblock on their noses. They said they would be back for dinner and my mother held my head by the ears and kissed my hairline. I thought she might have said something, but I couldn't tell because she had my ears covered.

I met Janice on the first formal night. I was wearing a tie with little white stripes and she had fallen into the wall in front of me after the ship hit a particularly big wave. She'd broken her sparkly high heel and I could bend it the wrong way like a broken arm. I told her to wait and I ran back to my room with the circular window and grabbed glue I had brought with me to finish a project where I had to stick the names of cities in Greece onto a colourful map. I glued Janice's heel back in place and she thanked me for getting her back on her feet.

The next day I saw her sunbathing on the top deck. She had untied her halter bathing suit so her tan would be even. I walked by her on the track that circled the top floor. Janice pushed her sunglasses up onto her head and when I said hello I could see her face was getting burnt. "Your face is getting burnt," I said.

"Oh, that's okay. It always turns into a tan," she replied. "Hey, Daddy. This is the boy that fixed my shoe."

Her father was suntanning beside her and his back was hairy. He flipped over and reached an oily hand my way. I grabbed it and smiled.

"What are your plans for the day?" I asked them.

"We're going to head to the spa. Have you been?"

Janice was speaking to me with a sort of indifference that made me interested in her.

"My mother's been going every day for a massage after she runs on the treadmill," I said. "It's not really my thing though. I find it pretty hard to relax." Janice's father looked at me like he didn't understand the anxieties of an eighteen-year-old kid. His skin had taken on the texture of my favourite leather jacket and his shoulders were starting to bubble.

"Well, I'll see you around, I guess," I said. I got jammed in an elevator with a bunch of people dressed for different activities: bathing suits, running shoes, fancy dresses and goggles. The whole thing made me feel anxious. When I got back to my room I stared at the school books I had piled beside a mirror that was always lit up. There was an itinerary on the bed beside a hand towel folded into a swan. I put the swan on the beside table, making sure that it kept its shape. I lay on the bed and looked at the itinerary. There was a hypnotist in the piano bar at noon and a comedy show in the great hall at eight. There was fitness cycle in the gym at three and a belly-flopping contest at the main pool at four.

I stared out my small circular window. All I could see was sky. My mother had passed on her red hair to me, so I could never tan the way Janice could. Janice had her belly button pierced and a pink butterfly jewel hung down onto her stomach and grew greasy from the tanning oil. I pulled down my pants and started to think about Janice and her broken heel. I usually had a hard time fantasizing about anything when I masturbated, like I always knew when I was kidding myself. I hardly ever felt a wave from the ship, which was one of the weirdest parts about the whole cruising thing, that you forget you're doing it. But now the ship hit a wave and the force made the vessel dip sideways. I looked out the window and for a second I could see water. After the ship stabilized, I realized I had cum at the same time the wave hit. I grabbed the towel and killed the swan.

Nora

My husband had taken me on a cruise years ago, right after we were married. I had feigned excitement but I hated being at sea, something I wished he'd known. I grew up on Bell Island and you needed to take a ferry there. Cars lined up for the ferry on both sides and wrapped around the hill like a blanket until they were ushered on by a man whose middle name they knew. This was the thing about Bell Island, everyone knew everyone. When I was a kid, the ferry made me sick as a dog. I would rock back and forth until I could hear the boat hitting rocks and then I would know the end was near. When I was growing up, all the men worked on the boat or in the mines. The mines ran underneath the ground like veins and everyone was happy. When the mines closed, thousands of people moved off the island but my family stayed. My dad got a job driving the taxi and eventually took over Esso oil. My parents had eight boys before me and they all worked for Dad. They would go to town and fill up the trucks and bring the oil back to the island. They would keep people warm in the winter.

Robert insisted we move to town. He hated Bell Island, he said it made him feel claustrophobic like he was getting an MRI or something. I told him I often felt like that too. Like people were looking at us too closely, like they could see inside us, to our brains. When we finally moved off the island, I vowed to only go back when I had to.

Now my parents had taken us on another cruise. They said that they had always wanted to go, it had been a dream. They had been jealous when Robert and I had gone years ago, so now they were paying and they encouraged us to bring Hugh, so we all got our passports renewed and bought new sunscreen. The cruise reminded me of home in all the worst ways. I kept running into the same people, my parents were in the room next to mine, and we were surrounded by water on all sides.

"Honey, just relax," Robert said. We had a room with a balcony and he was out there with his feet up. Hugh was two floors below us with his own room, which felt odd considering he still lived at home. He seemed further away than ever. We would eat breakfast together in the mornings and Hugh and I would get our omelettes made in the same pan by a man named Raphael.

I sat beside Robert on the balcony and told him this whole thing felt wrong. "You know the guy that makes our omelettes?" I put my hair in a ponytail now that it was long enough. "He has to leave his family in the Philippines for six months at a time!" Robert was staring ahead like he wasn't bothered. "So he can sprinkle parsley in my omelette while the egg cooks. Isn't that madness?"

"Honey, it's his job. He probably likes it," Robert said.

I had been thinking of all the late nights Robert had been working at his new restaurant. After he told his staff he was going on a week-long cruise, he told me, he had gone into the staff washroom and cried, consumed with guilt. I had been messaging a man named Max online who lived in Corner Brook. We had gone to high school together on Bell Island and he had found me on Facebook. I always made sure to delete the emails after they were sent, since Robert and I shared a laptop. Max and I would stay up late emailing and I would pour myself a glass of red wine to the rim. We would talk about how terrible it was, growing up in a place so solitary, and I would talk about my brothers.

"Remember we would go to those parties at Lance Cove beach and see how far we could swim out until our parents got mad."

I was always surprised at Max's memory. It made me like him. He had all these memories saved up like a database and it made me feel close to someone while Robert was at work. When my parents insisted on the cruise, Robert had made love to me for the first time in months. He told me he was excited to reconnect. All I could think about was the water.

Hugh

For as long as I can remember, my mother has marked her upcoming period on the family calendar with a red marker. Sometimes I think about little things like this and appreciate my mom for her organization—her follow-through. My parents and I lived in a baby-blue house on Coronation Street. My buddy Kyle told me in September that he was renting a two-bedroom place on Duckworth but my parents had convinced me to stay home.

"You don't need to spend money on rent. We have a perfectly good house here," my father had said, like I would be a fool to consider an option that didn't involve them. My father had just opened an oyster bar on Water Street and it was mostly very popular, but it meant he was never home. My mother, usually disciplined and pessimistic in a way that I appreciated, had turned giddy. She would go to bed early and kiss me on the ear before I heard her bedroom door close. Sometimes I'd hear her laugh and return to the kitchen to refill her glass. My parents' wedding photo sat above our TV. In the picture, my mother's dress was an off-white, which she swears she didn't know until the pictures were developed. Her head was buried in my dad's shoulder and she was smiling. They looked young and unlined.

I wondered why my grandparents had taken just us on the cruise and not their other kids. When I asked my grandfather over puréed asparagus soup one night at dinner, he told me the boys were busy.

"They have a business to run," he said. It started off as his business and it was assumed that the boys would take it over. My mother was free of this responsibility.

"I'm happy you don't have to do that work, sweetie," my grandmother said to me.

My mother was a therapist. She had an established list of clients and for years, her money was our family's only source of income. Because my mother's work wasn't physically exhausting, her brothers always talked about her having it easy. If it wasn't for my grandfather, I feared that the whole place would go to the dogs. My grandfather wielded a certain power over the family—he was the glue that kept everyone in place—like the glue that kept Janice's heel from falling off. He kept people's heads on their shoulders.

Janice

I met Hugh on Deck Eleven while everyone else was on land. He was holding two cones of soft serve, one chocolate and one vanilla. I grabbed the vanilla from him and felt the cream melt off the cone and onto my hand. We went to the arcade. It was the darkest room on the ship. We played a game with big fake orange guns and Hugh killed me first. I accidentally hit his soft serve out of his hand and it landed on the floor upside down: a puddle of ice cream getting bigger as we stared at it.

We walked through the promenade holding hands and Hugh told me he thought it would be cool if we took elevators on opposite sides of the ship and watched each other as we went up. The elevators were all glass and I watched as Hugh's elevator kept stopping to let people in. Mine shot all the way to the top and I pressed my nose against the glass until it was flat, and waved at Hugh, who was smiling. On the top floor we crossed our arms on the railing and looked out at the sea. There was no land around us and I asked Hugh if he liked cruising.

"I don't know. It's okay. It's weird that everything is so organized for you. I guess some people like that. I'm actually surprised my mom isn't having a better time. She's such a planner. I thought she would appreciate someone else doing the work." He turned around. "I guess maybe she misses being the one with the answers."

Hugh had floppy red hair that he kept touching and he had a big nose but there was something very cute about him, something innocent.

"I don't think my parents are very happy being married to each other," Hugh said. "Actually I think my mom is having some sort of affair."

"Really?"

"Yeah." He was still leaning against the railing and part of me wanted to take a photo of him. "And you know what else is so weird. Like this ship is called Carnival Freedom. But like there's Carnival Glory and Carnival Triumph and Carnival Liberty. What kind of fucking names are those?"

He suddenly seemed upset and I didn't really know why so I just nodded.

"Like do people believe that if they spend a week being like glorious or triumphant or liberated or free, they're going to feel better about their lives?"

My back was against the railing now and I looked back at the Carnival Freedom. There were two large green and blue slides that twisted and wrapped around each other like braids. Kids were sliding down them with their arms above their heads.

"I think maybe people do feel better," I said. "You know, some people just believe what you tell them. If they're spending a week on the Carnival Freedom they might just feel free."

"That's bullshit," Hugh said. I thought it was too, but I wasn't going to say it wasn't real. I wanted to hug Hugh and knock the sadness out of him and watch it pool around our feet.

Hugh and I went back to his bedroom and we lay on his bed wrapped around each other like the slides on the top deck. We talked about feeling free and how it was for suckers. I stared out his window and all I could see was sky. He asked me about growing up in Texas and I told him I never saw the water. I told him he was lucky that he lived on an island and that it must make him feel free. But he said it didn't make him feel like that.

Nora

I was walking the track, becoming more and more comfortable with the boredom it brought me and how it distracted me from the anxiety of being at sea.

"Miss?" A man in a Carnival Freedom personnel tank top tapped me on the shoulder. I could see the hair under his arm and I thought a T-shirt would have been more professional. I removed the headphones I was wearing and noticed that I was out of breath. The sun was hot above us and now that I was standing still, I could feel the boat moving underneath my feet.

"Whoa. Rocky today, sir," I said. The man was holding a tray of strawberry daiquiris in his left hand. I wiped my forehead with the back of my hand and grabbed a daiquiri from the tray, telling the man I was impressed with his balance.

"You are Miss Doyle?" he asked. "Your father is in Medical down on the second floor, miss. He tried to jump overboard this morning after brunch at the Winchester." He looked at me closely, like he was waiting for me to react. "However, he landed in a lifeboat, so he should be okay."

The daiquiri slid out of my sweaty hand and spilt all over my white tennis shoes. He led me to Medical on the second floor and I breathed heavily the whole way. When I got there, my father was sitting in a bed with pink and blue blankets, looking smaller than I'd ever remembered him looking. I pushed the hair off his forehead and instead of asking why he jumped overboard, I paid the roaming charges and Googled it on my phone instead. Google said that it was very common for people to jump off cruise ships. It happened all the time! I wondered if the ship was reminding him of Bell Island too. After a while, Robert came rushing into Medical. He had a visor with sunglasses on top. He had a pina colada in his hand and it was spilling everywhere as he ran.

"What happened? Are you okay? Someone came to find me. I was asleep on the top deck."

"Shhhh," I said quietly so he would stop talking and I turned back toward my father. I felt Robert put his arms around my shoulders and wrap his hands around my front, under my breasts. His forearms were sticky with sunscreen and the whole thing felt suffocating.

That night, after tucking my mother into bed, I told Robert I was going for a walk. He asked where and he reminded me there was nowhere to go. I grabbed the laptop and tucked it under my arm. I had never felt so compelled to speak to Max. I emailed him from the hotspot in the promenade that felt eerie when it was completely devoid of people. I messaged saying my father had jumped off the ship and landed in a life-boat. I typed *HAHA* afterwards and then deleted it. I couldn't figure out if the situation was funny or tragic or both. I hadn't seen Hugh since our morning omelette and I felt like avoiding him forever if it meant I never had to tell him about his grandfather. Max sent something back in seconds, the email coming through with the small ding of a child's bicycle bell. "Can I call you?" the email said. I told him yes and when he called his voice came through quietly, reminding me he was very far away. "I wish I could be there with you," he said.

I hadn't yet allowed myself to cry and suddenly I found myself sobbing onto the keyboard in the middle of the prome-nade. Tears fell off my face and leaked between the keys. Max let me cry until I could stop and I realized the phone call would be charged to my room.

"I didn't know he was so unhappy," I said.

I could hear Max thinking on the other end and I felt closer to him than I did to anyone on the ship.

"Maybe he's not. Maybe he's just tired of being at sea." It sounded like Max was eating a chip on the other end of the line and I wondered what flavour. "We should try to see each other when you're back."

I knew then that I would end my marriage. "You're a life-saver," I whispered. I thought about the idea of jumping off something big into something else that floats.

Hugh

When I was eight, I begged my parents for a goldfish. So my mother took me to the PetSmart on Stavanger Drive and I picked one out from the tank. A tall teenager with lots of pimples on his face handed me a large plastic bag filled with water and a goldfish inside. When he asked what I would name it, I said I would name it Hugh.

"Why are they called goldfish if they're orange?" I asked my mother, and she didn't respond. She just clicked the new electronic thing on our keys that unlocked the Ford Explorer. I sat in the front seat. My dad had just started letting me do that the week before. I fastened the seatbelt and held the bag with the fish up in front of my face and stared at it all the way home. As my mom drove by St. Clare's hospital she ran a red light and T-boned a small silver car heading downtown. I screamed until the airbag knocked the wind out me. My mother reached a hand toward me and one of her fingers got bent the wrong way. I stared ahead in shock and then I felt wet. I looked down and wondered what had happened and then I remembered the goldfish. I was small enough to slide out of the seat, even with the inflated airbag, so I opened the door and crawled out onto the pavement.

"Mom! I can't find the fish!" I was screaming and sweating and my body was still in shock. I couldn't really feel the ground. "Mom! The fish! I can't find it!" I lay flat on my stomach and saw the fish under the car flopping around uncontrollably. I reached out and grabbed it in my hand and I held it there in my fist as I realized the commotion around me. The paramedic ended up giving me his full Nike water bottle and it wasn't until I saw the fish swimming again that I could breathe easy. My mother had broken her finger and she needed stitches on her forehead. I was mostly fine but I would never forget that day.

That night my father prodded my mother for details about the accident. He had been home having a nap when it happened and he hadn't been answering his cellphone. His joblessness at the time had become a real strain on my mother. I knew that because she told me so. My mother believed in honesty and fairness and discipline.

"Do you think this fish is like us? He can only survive when he's surrounded by water, right?"

My mother was clearing off her plate into the garbage and balancing it awkwardly because of the finger. My father didn't offer to help her, which I always remembered.

"Yeah, honey. He's exactly like us."

At ten o'clock, there was a knock on my door. The boat was rocky that night and I felt queasy. When I answered, my mother stood there looking small and sad. Her face was red and I couldn't tell if it was a burn. She had fair skin and freckles and she thought she could be out in the sun for longer than was safe.

"Do you want to go for a walk, Hugh?"

"Yeah, sure." I bent down so I could see her eyes. "Are you okay?"

She looked up and I saw that she had been crying. We went to the top deck, to the fancier pool with the slide. The lights underwater made everything seem pink. We sat on the edge of the pool and put our feet in the water.

"Your grandfather jumped off the boat this morning," my mother said when we were sitting beside each other, our thighs touching.

I moved my foot and it created a splash. "What?"

"He landed in one of the lifeboats hanging off the side of the ship. He's going to be fine. He's in Medical on the second floor."

I stared at the water as it moved around my foot. "Mom, imagine if he had died. Everything would have fallen apart."

"I know. He's the glue," she said.

I jumped in the pool then even though I was in all my clothes. I needed to be underwater. Everything was pink around me. I held my breath for as long as I could and then I came up for air.

BAD ENDING

Willow and Meg starting fasting in the spring. They were in lockdown and there was nothing better to do.

"I'm just feeling incredibly uninspired to make art," Meg said. "And if I can't make anything then I need another project. So maybe I'll try to lose some weight."

This made Willow think about productivity and her weight loss from the summer before. "Yeah, I mean when Trevor broke my brain, I just started climbing Signal Hill every day because it felt like the only thing I could do most days. I was so afraid of losing him that I would just walk up and down the hill and take voice memos of all the things that scared me the most."

"Did you like plan to lose weight though when you started doing that?" Meg was drinking her second coffee of the day and had spilt some on the collar of her new polo from the thrift store. Black coffee was all they could drink until dinner.

"No, I think it just started happening because I was so anxious all the time, so I couldn't really eat anything. But I remember when I gained some weight in high school, I had this big conversation with my parents where they told me they were scared of me getting too big. So when I started getting smaller, it was kind of like an added bonus. Get sad, get hot!" Willow said the last part as a joke but it hung in the air in a way that made her feel bad for herself.

"Aren't your parents like afraid of everything, though?" Meg said as she loudly slurped the end of her black iced coffee—the light-brown coffee that drips down between the ice and becomes hard to get at.

Willow laughed. "Yeah, I remember in high school they would hear something on the news about packaged deli meat or oatmeal or whatever and how it was bad for you, and from that point forward it wasn't allowed in the house."

"That's so crazy to me. My mom never gave a shit about what I ate growing up." Meg's parents had divorced when she was a kid. Whenever she talked about it, she said them getting divorced was great. A COD, she called herself proudly. Child of Divorce. Why would you stay with somebody who makes you unhappy? she would say. That's no way to live. Nothing seemed to scare Meg. She was tough and ready for life in a way that made Willow feel weak sometimes. Willow remembered Trevor telling her once that life felt harder for him. Like the edges of his life were sharp and scary. When he started taking Zoloft the summer they broke up, he said the edges softened. Everything became less scary, to the point where he didn't know what was real. Willow opened the voice memo function on her phone and said this thought out loud.

That night Willow fell asleep finishing *The Girl with the Dragon Tattoo*. Falling asleep to a book that was so deliberately disturbing assured her she was exhausted. She remembered avoiding the book years ago when it was a huge phenomenon. She couldn't figure out if she did things when she was supposed to or if it was the other way around. She waited until she was twenty-five to engage in a relationship with a man. She didn't smoke or do drugs growing up. She had two degrees by the time she was twenty-three. She was too scared of what would happen if she lived precariously. By being a perfect overachiever, she didn't get any of the messy stuff out of her system because of fear. She was sensitive and obsessive: a bad combination.

The whole next day she thought about fear. And our responses to fear can be read by others in opposite ways from how we really feel. She'd always presented such a strong front but lately she'd been thinking about the discrepancy between how peopleunderstood her and how she really felt. So many times she didn't act in her own interest was because she was scared. She'd messaged Trevor when the lockdown was first announced and told him she was scared of not having structure—of being too free from school and jobs and the people she loved. She needed things to hold onto. She understood that fear more than anything else was an outlook, a framing, an experience more than a truth. But it didn't matter if the fear was in response to a genuine threat or a perceived one—the experience was the same. This made her think about Trevor and the sharp and scary edges. What was actually sharp didn't really matter.

She wanted to get beyond fear! She wanted to be post-fear! She wanted to be more like Meg. She wondered if she could change her responses. It wasn't until recently that she realized she was a control freak. She needed information about what was to come, so she could prepare herself and shape the outcome.

That weekend, Willow and Meg sat on their roof. Their property management company had removed their deck at the end of the previous summer when water started seeping into the kitchen in big, sad, beige stains. Now they were forced to lie on the roof, where the black tar ruined Meg's new puffer jacket from Uniqlo.

"Do you have Co-Star?" Meg asked. Co-Star was a social media app where information about people was catalogued according to their star sign and chart. Meg had recently broken up with her boyfriend, Gord, and she was using theories about their respective charts to justify how they weren't a great match all along.

"No I don't have it, I always forget what time I was born."

"Oh my God, dude, text your mom and find out."

Willow's mom texted her back right away. "10:30 p.m. Happiest night of my life xo."

She and Meg were both Leos. She checked their compatibility chart. "It says here that you need a lot of love, care and validation from other people," Willow said to Meg before applying sunscreen to her face. She was always scared of getting burned. "But I don't think you're like that."

"Mmmm I can be," Meg said. "I don't know. I've been thinking about fasting and it's just taking over my brain in this weird way."

"You know, it's strange because most people talk about losing weight but you've never really talked about it before," Willow said. "Anytime I've been insecure you've told me that I have to learn to love myself and shit like that."

Meg laughed. Her laugh was always bigger than Willow was expecting.

"I know," Meg said. "I do worry that people are going to think I'm being hypocritical by fasting. I just feel like lost or something. I don't know, it's hard to explain."

Willow didn't respond for a while. Fasting was scary. She'd finally figured out how to eat after a lifetime of disordered eating and now she was throwing off her routine. It made her feel out of control again, which she hated. She looked up at Meg and saw that she was crying slightly. The sun was beating down on them for the first time in ages in St. John's and it all felt weird and unreal. The light was obstructing Meg's face so Willow couldn't see it clearly.

"Meg, no one thinks you're a hypocrite. You're the strongest person I know."

Meg smiled faintly and Willow noticed then that she'd lost some weight in her face. Her angles were sharper.

"I feel empty," Meg said. "I'm hungry."

Willow agreed, but they didn't eat.

That night, Willow clocked into her serving job at five-thirty. The restaurant was at limited capacity and everyone was walking on eggshells. There were plastic partitions between people at communal tables that were meant for sharing. Willow was wearing a thick linen mask she'd bought at the mall and she could feel a pimple developing by her nose. Everyone seemed scared to be in public. People didn't know how to touch each other anymore. Willow snuck down to the staff bathroom in the basement even though she didn't have to pee. She opened her phone to a news alert saying that the remains of 215 children had been found buried near a residential school in BC. She double-clicked her home button and swiped up to exit the page.

Willow finished *The Sopranos* at the start of the week. The series, which she'd been watching since the last lockdown, ended with a black screen. Journey's "Don't Stop Believin'" gets cut short and the viewer is supposed to project their own idea of what happened onto the ending. The whole thing made Willow angry. She thought it was a cop-out for the writers to leave the audience with no tangible ending.

"I finished *The Sopranos*!" she yelled as she emerged from her bedroom for the first time all night. Her roommate Poppy was lying on the couch with her feet on her boyfriend Fred's lap. Meg was sitting on the other couch painting her toenails the colour of grass and eating hummus on a rice cake. Poppy was drawing on the iPad that her parents had given her for Christmas. Willow remembered last winter when their cat, Turtle, had run around the room with Poppy's iPad pen in its mouth and Poppy yelled about how it had cost two hundred dollars.

"What did you think of the ending?" Fred asked. He'd been essentially living at their house and it was definitely his turn to buy toilet paper.

"I don't know. It was kinda bullshit."

"Yeah. I feel like it couldn't have ended any other way though. Like it was cool in that it was kind of a rejection of an end or whatever," Fred said. Fred was wearing a Foo Fighters hat and had been born in 2000. In some ways Willow felt lucky to live with someone so young. He felt fresh and unencumbered by things that hurt. He wasn't optimistic, but he had a certain faith in things that Willow seemed to have lost.

Willow and Trevor were still talking most days even though she'd seen him with a blond girl outside Bannerman Park last Tuesday. She knew that she was keeping this flame burning because she was rebelling against an ending. For a long time she thought that she was self-protective, that she feared endings so much that she prepared for them. She would end things prematurely as a way of holding onto control.

"I mean think about it," Fred said. "They're not going to give you the satisfaction of seeing Tony die. You have to decide for yourself how the end is going to affect you."

"Yeah and the good thing is, Willow, is it's not really over. I mean it might be, because James Gandolfini is dead, but look at *Friends*. I was in H&M yesterday and there were just like T-shirts and sweatpants with the *Friends* logo on them. And like the characters' names and shit like that. It's so weird, like why can't people grow up?"

Willow laughed and said something about romantic nostalgia and how people, especially in America, always return to what they know.

"I mean the *Sopranos* finale is called 'Made in America,'" Fred said before licking Zesty Dorito cheese off his index finger. "I just think we're so doomed if all we do is repurpose the same stories from our youth over and over again. I just saw Netflix is animating a show called *Velma* based on the *Scooby Doo* character."

Willow stood up to get a Black Horse from the fridge and saw that Poppy was drawing a poster on her iPad that she was planning to sell that weekend at the Eastern Edge Print Fair. The app she used to draw was called Procreate. Poppy's drawings were all images from Phoebe Bridgers's new album

Punisher. There was a graphic in the bottom left corner that said *The End is Near*.

Willow was reading a book called *Betrayal* for a class she was taking at MUN.

"The covers of these books are really something," Meg said as she joined Willow on the roof and started smoking.

"The main character in this book won't stop smoking either," Willow said. "It's actually funny, the girls in the book like get together and smoke on the balcony at their work. Them smoking is like the only peaceful time in the book. When they stop smoking and go inside they have to be scared again or something. It's like a reprieve from the world."

Meg had quit smoking over the winter, except for sometimes one after dinner. But since they had started fasting, Meg seemed to be renegotiating her relationship to it.

"Do you ever think about smoking being bad for you?" Willow said. "I feel like any time I smoke I'm just completely inundated with this feeling of guilt. It's like not worth it."

"I don't know. I guess I just don't really think about it like that. It's almost like if I can't see the harm it's doing to me then it doesn't matter," Meg said. "I feel like you have more of a mortality mindset than I do."

"What do you mean?"

"I don't know. I think it might be Trevor, honestly. He's just so depressing and sad and he wants to die all the time so it's made you less inclined to live."

Meg always said things in this concise way that ignored the context. Willow thought it was kind of a skill.

Since breaking up with Gord, Meg seemed to be doing better than ever. "Listen, an ending is a loss, and everything ends and everything's temporary, but most things don't have what feels like a prescribed ending. Like friendships and relationships, barring some unforeseen drama or betrayal, aren't something you expect to expire." Meg started talking about Gord and how it was the right thing for them to end their relationship.

"Well, that's what's so interesting about these books that I'm reading for this class. It's like this kind of one-sided extension of something is interesting. Like the remembering of something keeps it from ending."

Willow thought about one of the last episodes of *The Sopranos*. Tony and Pauly go to Las Vegas to hide from the feds and Pauly won't stop reminiscing about the past. Tony eventually leaves the table angrily and says, "'Remember when' is the lowest form of conversation." Willow thought about all the relationships in her life that were kept alive by the past. She knew it wasn't always a bad thing, but people's inability to let go and move on in meaningful ways kept them from moving forward.

Meg was playing Killer Sudoku on her phone now, her cheeks getting red in the sun.

"Something that's funny about these books too is how much infidelity is in all of them," Willow said.

"Ah yes, an ending without actually having to end anything."

Willow and Poppy went to the new sex store that was opening on Water Street. Their friends were selling erotic literature and vibrators out of a hole in the wall that used to sell records. Poppy was talking about how she was going to school in Toronto in September.

"I just don't know what to tell Fred." She was drinking a vanilla sweet cream cold brew from Starbucks and walking slower than Willow would like. Poppy never said too much, but she was one of the smartest people Willow knew. She absorbed everything around her and she felt everything, in big and hard ways. "I've just been in relationships before and I know how catatonic you can feel when they end," Poppy said. "But Fred's never had that happen before. I don't want to be the first person to like break his brain or whatever."

"But are you guys going to stay together while you're in Toronto?"

"I don't know, maybe. That like in-between, purgatory relationship is actually hell and just will prevent either of us from living separate lives fully."

When they got to the sex store, Poppy picked out a cow-print vibrator.

"Are you getting one?" she asked Willow.

"It might be a waste of money," Willow said. "You know I can't finish."

VALUE

Amber's father took her to buy a second-hand car when she turned seventeen. He said he would co-sign and she would have to make monthly payments for the insurance. She was considering universities and suspected the car was a tactic to convince her to stay in Guelph. Amber and her father drove up to Woodlawn Road and went so far they were almost in Cambridge. There was a man with a handlebar moustache at Honda who tried to sell them a second-hand Civic. He got in the front seat and put his hand on the wheel like he thought Amber would immediately want to imitate him. Amber and her father both bent over slightly to see him do this and then Amber told him she would take it.

"What's she worth?" Amber's father asked and she thought that unless this guy was from Newfoundland too, he wasn't going to understand what this meant.

"Sorry, sir, how much is who worth?"

"The car!"

"Oh, well, it's valued at about ten, but I'll give it to you guys for eight," he said and he winked at Amber, which made her shudder.

Amber walked outside to the middle of the lot. There was a hatchback sitting on a platform and Amber wondered how it got there. The windshield was painted like a rainbow and it said HALF OFF in block letters that drew the eye. Amber could see all the way down Woodlawn to the Guelph Galaxy.

The week before at their high school's semi-formal, Amber's friend Mary had drunk a full twenty-sixer of cherry vodka straight from the bottle with a twirly straw. Then Mary had puked all over the new strapless dress her mother had found her at the BCBG in the Eaton Centre. She wiped the puke off with toilet paper and said she was fine to go to the formal. Their friend Kelly, who wasn't drinking because she had field hockey in the morning, pulled over into the parking lot of the Guelph Galaxy when Mary passed out in the back. Kelly was driving her mother's Range Rover with the new entertainment headrests so her younger brothers could watch Marvel movies when the family went for long drives. Amber and her best friend Erin laid Mary flat behind the back door of the theatre. Star Wars was showing at the Galaxy at eight-thirty and Amber saw a father and his son entering the theatre with their own Doritos. Mary started choking on her vomit so they rolled her on her side. There was dirt all over Mary's new cream dress with the bow at the front.

"I'm not fucking dealing with this," Erin said.

"Well, you don't have a choice. We're not going to leave her here," Amber answered, and wrapped her shawl around Mary like she was tucking her in.

The G in Galaxy was burnt out but the rest of the letters shone down on the girls as they all bent over Mary, who could only moan. Kelly said she would drop the girls at the formal and take Mary to emergency. Mary shook her head when Kelly said this and the girls picked Mary up by her arms and legs.

When Kelly dropped the girls at the hall, Amber suddenly felt cold and she wanted her shawl. She wanted to be wearing sweatpants and she wanted to be at a movie. Their high school had started breathalyzing at the door of the formal and two cops stood outside smoking cigarettes.

After they served sliced chicken breasts on a bed of rice, everyone was encouraged to dance. Erin grabbed Amber's hand and told her she thought the DJ was cute. All Amber could smell was the vodka on Mary's dress. It was stuck in her nostrils forever, it seemed. Amber moved her hips and her shoulders to the music and Erin grabbed her hands and put them over her head. All Amber's friends snuck into the bathroom to chug spiced rum they had taped to their underwear and Amber called her dad to pick her up. She waited outside for her father and her arms were cold.

"How was the dance, sweetie?" he said when she climbed into the front seat. He was wearing his softest sweater and his reading glasses, which meant he had been in bed when she called. Amber started to cry and her shoulders shook up and down like they did when she was dancing.

"Honey, you ready to go? You're a car owner!" her father yelled from the door of the dealership, pulling Amber out of her head.

Amber turned around and gave him a thumbs-up and then she yelled thank you and he smiled like she was thanking him for the Civic.

That summer, Amber had started dating her friend Luke. They had known each other since they were kids and shared a neighbourhood bus stop. Amber had always been really good friends with Luke's sister but now when she went over to their house, she didn't know how to manage her time. They usually went to Luke's room after Amber said hi to his parents. Luke's mom would usually pull her into a hug and talk about how she remembered when Amber was just a kid. And when they would get up to Luke's room he would try to undo her bra through her shirt. Luke had a basketball net hanging above his door and tiny rubber basketballs dispersed across his floor like socks. Sometimes he would lie on his back with her on his chest and he would shoot baskets while they talked. He had mastered the shot that allowed the ball to roll back onto the bed and into his hands so he didn't have to move.

"What is Erin doing anyway?"

"I don't know, she's like up at her chalet or whatever."

Erin had been Amber's best friend since middle school. Her parents were part of an elite ski club up north and they drove two hours every Friday afternoon to get there. In the summer they used the chalet as a cottage. Erin's parents were both lawyers and they worked at the same firm. Amber had gone to the ski club once and twisted both ankles on a double black diamond, so she never went back.

"Is she coming back for the party?" Luke asked, and he ran his hands through Amber's hair, which felt nice.

Amber's arms were crossed on Luke's collarbone and she leaned up and kissed him on the chin. "Yeah, as if she would miss that."

Luke and his hockey team were having a bush party to fundraise for matching tattoos of hockey sticks on their arms.

"Dude, we're gonna make so much money."

"Where is it anyways?"

"Southvale," Luke said and then rolled Amber off him. They lay beside each other on his Toronto Maple Leaf sheets that smelled like sweat. They hadn't had sex yet and Amber was terrified. She always wore her best underwear when she went to Luke's and she shaved her legs. When she thought about being that close to someone though, she felt short of breath. The thought of lying to her parents and doing things they wouldn't approve of made her feel like someone was stepping on her lungs. She stood up and shot a basketball into the hoop.

"You should go pro," Luke said and squeezed her hip as she put her shoes on.

That night when she got home from Luke's, Amber could hear her parents talking in the kitchen. She stood in the doorway of the living room so they couldn't see her.

"There's just no way we can pay for this right now," her mother said, and Amber thought about the down payment on the Civic. She looked at the table and both her parents' backs were toward her. Her father was leaning over her mother, rubbing small circles on her back. Her father was a financial adviser at the Royal Bank and Amber thought there was something funny about him advising other people on their finances when his weren't together.

Her family had been following the American election and they would watch the debates together with popcorn. Whenever the moderator asked a question about the financial crash, Amber's father would shake his head and talk about how those guys got away with murder.

"We'll be fine. The kids may have to get jobs and we'll probably have to take out another mortgage on the house if Amber wants to go to school, but that's okay."

Amber wanted to reach out and hug her dad until he couldn't breathe. She wanted to give back the Civic if it meant he could sleep at night. She never wanted to tell him that she and Erin both talked about Montreal and how Concordia was her first choice for school. She went to a private school and everyone had money. Their parents bought the expensive hummus with the pine nuts and they all had glass cabinets with lots of liquor bottles lined up inside. Every weekend since her friends started drinking, Amber would find herself at a different house party where she would be drinking wine out of a red plastic cup beside a pool with a rock floor. The lights from the pool would illuminate the backyard and country music would play from the ten-thousand-dollar sound system inside. The ping-pong table would be pulled out onto the grass in the backyard so everyone could play beer pong. The guys would get so drunk that they would stumble around the backyard and sometimes they'd fall.

Erin had an overbite. Sometimes when she and Amber were alone she would see what she could stick between her top and her bottom teeth. A small tangerine, the table salt shaker, the remote control. When they were younger, it was funny, but as they got older it made Erin hate herself. Her parents took her to Oakville to see the best orthodontist in Southern Ontario, who told Erin on a consult that surgery would change her whole face. He said that she would need to have braces before they could break her jaw. Erin had laughed until she'd cried and suggested that maybe Amber should just break her jaw for her. She should punch her in the face, really hard until they heard a crack.

The bush party was that week, so Amber and Erin had driven to Toronto in Amber's car to get new outfits. They parked at Yorkdale and took the subway downtown so they didn't have to deal with traffic. When they got back to Erin's, her mother asked where the party was.

"Southvale," Amber said, even though she didn't know where that was exactly.

Erin's mother was making a spinach smoothie in her Vitamix. "Southvale isn't a residential road. It's the street with the factories that ends by the highway."

"Ugh, Mom, maybe it's like Southport or something, I don't know, it doesn't matter. We're staying at Mary's, so I'll call you in the morning." Erin kissed her mom on the cheek and Amber was amazed at how easily she could lie to her.

The girls gave Mary money and her brother bought them those individual mickeys of Smirnoff that they had started making in plastic bottles. They took a cab to the end of Southvale down a long dirt road. The factories were visible in the distance, their lights far away like stars. There was a low hum you could make out if it was quiet enough. The 401 was on the other side of them and the sound of transport trucks driving toward London got louder as they drove. Amber thought about how her father would be heading down the highway in a few hours. He had to drive to the bank headquarters in Toronto every week while it was still dark if he wanted to miss traffic. Mary handed the cab driver forty dollars and he shook his head like he didn't approve of where he was dropping them. There was a sign in blue writing on cardboard that had an arrow pointing toward the field. Erin started walking in the direction of the arrow in her new two-hundred-dollar jeans.

Wedged between the twenty-four-hour factory workers and the cross-country truck drivers were a bunch of rich kids partying. There was a clearing in the middle of the field that Luke and his friends had mowed that week. The boys had slung their parents' Christmas lights on some bushes and people were doing keg stands. There were multiple pairs of feet in the air at once.

Amber found Luke and his eyes looked empty with drunkenness. "Babe, this party is sick," he said, slurring.

Amber gave ten dollars to one of the guys with a fanny pack whose name was Lawrence. Lawrence was scary and terrible to girls and he dreamed of making it to the NHL. Amber sipped from her mickey of vodka and avoided the beer from the keg. Luke fell into her and whispered in her ear that the boys had filled the tops of the kegs with water. His breath was hot and she remembered when they were kids, playing road hockey on Luke's street down by their elementary school. She felt nostalgic for the clarity of their old relationship.

"You can't do that. You're ripping people off."

"Shhh," he said and put his hand over her mouth. It smelt like beer and sweat and she pulled it off.

Luke leaned toward her and said, "No one's gonna know. It's fine."

"Luke, you can't take people's money and then not give them what they asked for."

Luke squinted, too drunk to understand her. He smiled like he thought she was ridiculous when she was serious. He put his hand on her back and slipped it beneath the new tank top she had bought in Toronto that morning. A girl Amber didn't recognize bumped into them and knocked Amber's mickey out of her hand. It fell sideways on the ground and spilt into the grass.

"That was almost twenty dollars," Amber said to the girl and the girl laughed.

"COPS!"

A flashlight lit up Amber's face and made it hard for her to see.

"COPS!" she heard again and she felt Luke leave her side.

Everyone started running in every direction out of the field, like ants after their anthill had been stepped on. Amber turned and started sprinting toward the city. Luke was in front of her and he was fast even when he was drunk. Amber felt her camera fall out of her pocket, or maybe it was her phone, either way it was something valuable that she couldn't go back for. She kept chasing Luke and she pretended they were kids, playing hide-and-seek or tag. They finally got to the parking lot of their high school and Amber keeled over behind a dumpster trying to catch her breath. Luke turned around and picked her up and threw her over his shoulder. The cops weren't behind them and Amber wondered who they had caught.

"Luke, put me down, I'm serious!" Amber was hitting him on his back but he had all the control. Luke was laughing and Amber was terrified.

"You're always so serious!"

When he finally put her down she hit him in the stomach. "How can you be laughing right now!"

"C'mon, lighten up."

"We were almost just caught by the cops!" Everything came together in Amber's head to convince her that it was all wrong: the drinking, the bush party, the new clothes,

Luke wanting to have sex. It all seemed dirty to her now. "This isn't worth it," she said.

"Isn't worth what?" Luke seemed to have sobered up after the run. The lights from the school parking lot were shining down on them and lighting up Luke's face so she could finally see him.

"I don't know where Erin is, or Mary!"

"They're fine. Just chill."

"Does this seem worth it to you?"

"What?"

"All of this. What are we doing it for? Was it worth having that party so you could get a fucking tattoo of a hockey stick on your arm?" Amber was still breathing heavy. "I just don't see why we're doing all this stuff."

"We're doing it because it's fun," Luke said and he moved so he was out of the light.

"Getting chased by the cops isn't fun for me," Amber said. Her arms were waving, which was something that happened when she got angry. "I want to be serious. I want to think about my future."

"Well, great," Luke said. "Maybe you should move to Montreal and date a dude who buys you those long loaves of bread that you can't bite into. And you guys can speak French or whatever."

Amber and Luke hadn't really talked about her moving to Montreal and even if they weren't dating it would have been weird. They had never not been in each other's lives.

"You know, you really mean something to me," Luke said.

Amber wished he would quantify it more clearly but instead she just thanked him.

Erin got her jaw surgery at the end of the year. Her face was twice its usual size when Amber visited her in the hospital. The doctor said she couldn't eat solid food for six weeks so Erin blended meals her parents made into their Vitamix and sucked them through a straw at the table. They even set a place for her. When the doctor unwired her jaw, Erin had lost thirty pounds and gained everything else. She was pretty and people noticed. She started sleeping with the guys who used to tell her she looked like a horse, and the whole thing made Amber sad. She wanted things to mean something; she wanted people to suffer the consequences of their actions.

Amber's mom started selling running shoes downtown and told people how they could lose weight fast. Her parents sat her down with her brother and said they were having financial trouble. They said it wasn't anything to worry about, but Amber couldn't sleep until the end of the week. She got a job at Value Village and she started teaching herself graphic design through YouTube videos. She sold her favourite coat on Kijiji and got two hundred dollars for it. She gained weight in her face and felt undervalued. Everyone had sent in their applications for university except for a lot of the guys who wanted to stay back a year in high school. She thought they wanted more time to feel special.

Erin got into Concordia first and then Amber got in two months later. Erin accepted first even though it was all Amber's idea. The summer before they left for Montreal, Amber's car broke down and the engine smoked out. Her father called the dealership and said they hadn't got their money's worth. The dealership explained that the guy with the handlebar moustache—the one who gave them a deal—

didn't work there anymore. He wasn't telling the customers the truth, the man on the phone said.

On her father's advice, Erin took out a thirty-thousand-dollar loan before she moved to Montreal. She broke up with Luke and told him they didn't value the same things. He told her that she broke his heart and she patted him on the head and told him he would be okay. Before she moved away, she heard that he was making a killing selling weed.

Amber and Erin drove to Montreal in Erin's mom's hatchback with a U-Haul dragging behind them. On Kijiji, they found a place in the Mile End. It was falling apart but the rent was only three hundred and fifty each. They put a plant in the front window and they combined their books on a shelf in the living room. They went to IKEA and bought orange chairs for the kitchen and they sat on the back patio, which looked over a children's daycare.

"I guess we're growing up."

Erin started smoking a cigarette, which was something she was trying socially. She looked impossibly cool, Amber thought, but she didn't try one.

A week before they started school, Erin walked into the American Apparel on St. Denis and they asked her to model. When she got home that night she had five hundred dollars' worth of new crop tops and schoolgirl skirts.

"They said that I was exactly what they wanted. That I was pretty in a normal way."

"What does that mean?"

"I don't know. You've seen the ads. It's just like normal girls doing normal things." Erin put a bag of popcorn in the microwave and slammed the door really hard since that was the only way it would heat things up. "They're going to give me a thousand dollars a shoot. Isn't that crazy?"

Amber had transferred to the Value Village on Jean-Talon and had to take two buses and a subway there and still got paid minimum wage. "It's crazy." She hugged Erin and she could feel her bones through her back. She stuck her index finger between the top two and it made her feel closer to Erin until she pulled away.

That night, they shared the bag of popcorn in Erin's room while they watched *The Wire*. They went on Erin's Facebook and saw that Mary had sent them a message about how she felt lost without them in Guelph and she didn't have anyone taking care of her now. She sent a bunch of sad face emojis after that, and Erin minimized the conversation and called it a distraction. Amber went back to her room at midnight with greasy knuckles. She was mostly happy for Erin, that people were finally noticing that she was beautiful.

The next day, Amber biked to Value Village. When she got off her bike the neck of her T-shirt was soaked with sweat. She took long, laboured breaths as she locked her bike against the side of the building.

She went to the back room, where she was surrounded by piled clothes that people had given up. She put on the red vest with long pockets big enough for a forearm. Her co-worker Johnny was sitting on a floral couch that had a $29.99 price tag on the top and a white stain on the side. Johnny had headphones on and was listening to something that she could almost hear. He had a white cupcake on his lap with different coloured sprinkles and an unlit candle stuck in the middle. When he saw her, he pushed his headphones back so they were slung around his neck and she could hear that he had been listening to Zeppelin.

"Hey! I got this for you! Since you just started and all." She guessed Johnny was a few years older than her. He was tall and wore all black under his red vest. He told her on their last shift that he lived in Parc Ex and played the drums.

She took the cupcake from him and noticed it was on a plate that was on clearance a few days before. It was rimmed with small red flowers. "You really didn't have to do this. I'm serious. I did nothing to deserve it!"

Johnny laughed and said, "Really, Amber, it's my pleasure. It came in a pack of four and I'm going to eat those three later so really it's a gift for me."

She picked it up hesitantly because it looked like he wanted her to eat it. She took a big bite out of the side and Johnny wiped icing off her lip with his thumb.

She worked cash that afternoon and she felt full and happy.

"Excuse me. How much does this cost?" an older man with a lot of beige things in his cart asked her as he held up a sweater vest. "There's no tag."

Amber charged him $1.99 for it and felt good.

After work, Johnny and Amber biked to Place de la Paix for an outdoor screening of *The Good, the Bad and the Ugly*. Amber sat cross-legged and got a grass stain on her shorts. Johnny grabbed her hand and told her he'd always been a sucker for Westerns. Amber bought popcorn from a guy with a cart and she thought about Erin and how much she loved her. The sun went down behind the screen in different colours of orange, yellow and red, and Amber asked Johnny how much the movie cost. He told her it was free.

STANDBY

Kathleen sat down in the food court of Yorkdale mall, in front of Thai Express. She got New York Fries and pretended she was somewhere else. Arthur must have parked at the entrance by the Sears because he was coming up the escalator, more of him becoming visible as time passed, until she could see all of him. He was wearing khakis and that brown leather jacket she hated. He sat down across from her and wiped the crumbs off the table in front of him with his sleeve.

"You're late," Kathleen said.

He looked at his watch and said, "Barely."

Kathleen shook her head. "Do you want something to eat?"

"No, I'm okay."

"Are you sure? I don't want to eat if you're not eating anything."

"Well, I'm not hungry and you already bought food." He stole a fry soaked in gravy and popped it in his mouth before he dramatically exhaled. "Too hot," he said.

"Yeah, I'm letting them cool off. Do you remember you used to take me to the mall when we first met?"

"Yeah, and we would walk around and you would drag me to all these stores but you would never buy anything." He popped another fry in his mouth. "I always hated that."

Kathleen squinted at Arthur like he should have learned his lesson—that the fries were too hot—the last time. But this was the thing about Arthur, he wanted things to be hard. He took the divorce papers out of the long leather pocket she used to stick her hands in years ago to keep warm. He put the papers on the table and he grabbed another fry. A drop of gravy fell on the page, right over the words *irreconcilable differences*. He tried to rub it off, which only made it worse.

The spilt gravy drove Kathleen crazy. She hated things that were messy. Arthur knew this about her, which made his carelessness all the more insulting. "That's great, Arthur," she said.

Kathleen signed on the line with the arrow and her pen exploded. It went all over her hands and the mess spread everywhere.

Arthur worked for Air Canada and so did Kathleen. People always asked if they met in the air but it wasn't as romantic as that. They had met at the Avalon Mall when they were both based out of St. John's. They had both been at Winners looking for sheets to fit double beds. Kathleen was wearing her uniform and Arthur had asked where she was coming from.

"Oh, just a San Fran turn," Kathleen said, picking up grey sheets with the Ralph Lauren logo in the corner. They were for a queen-sized bed but they were on sale so Kathleen thought she could make them work—just a little extra fabric. "I'm Kathleen," she said, extending a hand.

"Arthur," he said. "You like the San Francisco?"

"Yeah. I mean, I used to bid for more overseas stuff but I'm finding lately that it's a lot of work since they've taken some crew out of the back."

"I'm a pilot," Arthur said.

Kathleen wondered how she didn't know him. He told her he'd transferred from Toronto after his divorce and then he picked up red sheets, which Kathleen was surprised by. They got a pretzel and shared it in the food court and when they walked to their cars, Arthur told her he was happy they met and she gave him her number.

Arthur and Kathleen had two boys in high school. Right before the divorce they all went on a family trip to Hawaii for March break. They travelled on employee passes and it took them three days to get there. Kathleen broke down at Gate 33 in the Pearson Airport and sobbed into her knees.

"This is exhausting. I'm exhausted, Arthur."

Their son Ben was asleep on the floor, his head on a backpack, lumpy with socks in the front pocket. And their son Andy was sitting beside them watching *Friday Night Lights* with headphones on.

"I don't know what you want me to do," Arthur said.

"It's like this every time."

"Yeah, well, you knew it was going to be like this. There's never any guarantee that we're going to get anywhere."

Kathleen wiped underneath her eyes and shook her head. "No, there's not," she said. Travelling standby was a specific kind of misery. Of course she and Arthur had flying privileges, but they never got anywhere unless there was room.

"Collins, party of four," was called from the gate and

Kathleen exhaled loudly. Arthur went up to get their boarding passes.

"We didn't get seats together," he said. "But we're on."

When they landed in Hawaii, the flight attendant put leis around their necks as they deplaned. They got off the plane onto the tarmac instead of the terminal. It was hot and the boys took off their sweaters and tied them around their waists. Arthur grabbed Kathleen's hand and kissed her on the cheek. She was sweating and she felt tired.

"Well, it took us three days, but we're here."

"Finally."

There were palm trees on the side of the runway and planes landing in the distance. Arthur could look up at a plane that was so high in the sky it was barely there, and he would know all the details about it. It was a skill of his that the boys always thought was impressive when they were younger.

"That's a 320, heading to Vancouver, Delta Airlines," he said looking up. All their heads craned upwards to look.

"Dad, there's like an app for that now." Ben pointed his iPhone at the sky and the plane details came through with a ding like a message. Arthur didn't say anything but Kathleen thought he looked hurt.

When they got to the hotel, Arthur told the boys that he was going to have a shower and would meet them at the pool. The boys changed into bathing suits and waited by the pool with their Nintendo Switches. When they left the room, Arthur kissed Kathleen like he hadn't in years and told her he missed her.

"I miss you too," Kathleen said and she meant it. She appreciated that he'd organized this trip and she appreciated that he missed her, but she felt terrible, like there was something pushing against her chest. Arthur put his hand on her chest and she pulled away and told him to stop it.

"Are you okay?"

Kathleen was backed against the wall that Arthur had pushed her against and she was breathing heavily. "I'm seeing someone," she said.

Arthur looked at her like he didn't understand. "What?"

"I met someone."

"What about the rules?"

"I broke them. I'm sorry."

A year before Hawaii, Arthur and Kathleen had decided to try an open relationship. They had sat down one night at the kitchen table with glasses of water filled to the top and then Arthur got a beer too. They talked about guidelines for this sort of thing and acknowledged that they were both unhappy but they didn't want to separate. They both wrote out rules that were important to them on pieces of lined paper that Kathleen had ripped out of Andy's math notebook. Her small cursive writing had five numbered points:

> *Rules for Open Relationship – Kathleen and Arthur*
> Set Boundaries
> No Emotional Attachment
> No talking about other partners to spouse
> Must disclose that you are married to other partners
> Always protect yourself (sexually+personally)

Arthur looked over the page and nodded his head like he agreed. "Are we sure about this?"

"I don't know, are we sure about anything?" Kathleen got up and poured herself tea in a mug Arthur had given her for their tenth anniversary. He had given it to her right after they had found out she was pregnant with Ben. That month they had also been notified that the St. John's flight attendant base was closing down. So they moved to Toronto and got a house in the Beaches. She remembered them being so happy then, like they could depend on each other.

Arthur had been the one to ask for the open relationship. Kathleen had cried that night in the bathroom and then taken two Gravols so she could sleep. They didn't discuss the idea again for weeks, until Andy broke his ankle at school and she met Arthur in emergency. He was late, like he always was, and he was in his uniform. He had just gotten back from a London. They sat beside each other in red plastic chairs and Kathleen said, "Do you just want to have sex with other people?"

"Kathleen—it's—"

"It's what?"

"Can we not talk about this here? Please."

There was a man across from them eating a sandwich with mayo and Kathleen wondered who he was waiting for and what his relationships looked like. The waiting room made her want to cry: the not knowing of it all. She needed answers from Arthur in a new way. She needed him to commit to the dismantling of their marriage or to their monogamous marriage. He didn't understand commitment and if he did he would make a decision. He would show up on time. He would think about the implications of his actions. The reason she didn't say all this had to do with one thing:

Arthur loved her. And he wanted her to be happy and he wanted their life together, when it was good.

When they got home, Andy was in a wheelchair. He asked how long until he was healed and Kathleen told him it could be a lifetime. Arthur rolled his eyes because he thought she was always more dramatic than she needed to be.

"Buddy, you should be fine to move in a month," Arthur said, ruffling Andy's hair until it stood up.

When Andy and Ben went to bed that night Kathleen said, "Okay, let's do it. But I want to know everything." She didn't realize this was already breaking the rules.

Two weeks later, Arthur slept with a flight attendant named Phoebe Klein on a layover to Paris. He told Kathleen over a beef stew she'd made without carrots, because Arthur hated them. The boys were at a sleepover and so Kathleen had lit candles. The first thing she thought when he told her was that she wished she'd added carrots.

"Remember when we were going to go to Paris?" Kathleen said, taking a bite of meat. "But we got trapped in Vancouver and it was so foggy that all the flights were cancelled."

"So we stayed in the airport hotel," Arthur said. "Yeah, I remember."

Kathleen wondered where everything had gone so wrong. She remembered when she and Arthur would look into each other's eyes for long periods of time. They would find hairs on each other's heads to play with. They would touch and they would moan. Happiness came to her late in life. She had grown up in St. John's and her best friend, Darcy, got engaged when they were twenty. Darcy and her high school boyfriend, Matt, had thrown a punk show to fundraise for their destination wedding to Mexico. Darcy had wanted to get married on an island and she wanted it to be warm. Kathleen reminded Darcy that she already lived on an island and that warm weather was coming up, even though it wouldn't last long. A bunch of their friends had played the show, which they threw at the Ship. People lined the stairs smoking until their eyes started to close. They had made enough money to cover their flights to Mexico and they got married on the beach with their shoes off. Darcy had worn flowers in her hair and that night their hotel gave them bed bugs. Darcy and Matt got divorced two years later when he told her he'd been sleeping with other people. Kathleen always felt like she was failing everyone around her by not finding someone named Matt or Mike and flying to Mexico to elope, so when Darcy got divorced it made her feel better, which she didn't say, she just assured Darcy she was better off.

Darcy and Matt's destination wedding made Kathleen wary of relationships until she met Arthur. Arthur was flawed but he was also transparent about his flaws. He was abrasive and honest and these things always made Kathleen sure that she understood him. When he asked for an open relationship, she hadn't seen it coming. She told Arthur it felt like turbulence, which he knew she hated. He didn't mind turbulence, though. In fact, he thought it was kind of fun. He would tell her turbulence was just like driving a car on a gravel road. It was nothing to be scared of.

She met Tony at Ben and Andy's high school. He was tall and shy, both things that Arthur was not. He was separated from his wife, who was blond and ran the children's bake-off every winter. Kathleen told him that she was in an open relationship and she felt sad and weird about it, and he told her that it was admirable that they weren't just giving up. He took her out to a bar around the corner from their children's school and Tony ordered them paper planes, which was an orange cocktail with amaro that made Kathleen feel loopy.

"Why are people in relationships?" Kathleen asked as she looked at Tony and started to feel drunk. "It seems to me that you have to be secure and trustworthy and sure to make anything work. And I don't know anyone who is sure about anything!"

Tony agreed with her and admitted that he always put way too much pressure on his wife to give him everything. "I was always like that though. When I didn't have the answers, I expected her to give them to me."

Kathleen had shaped their backyard in the Beaches so her plants lined the perimeter of the fence all the way to their neighbours' house. She would sit out there and water her plants any time she needed to be alone. Arthur resented how much time she spent out there and would comment on how the backyard had looked better when they moved in years ago.

"Why do you always make things so hard? I don't even know why you care about the backyard. You're never out here. This is something that makes me happy. Don't you want me to be happy?"

Arthur sleeping with Phoebe Klein had hurt her less than she thought. It was actually kind of liberating. After that she started telling Arthur exactly how she felt about everything, plus she started seeing Tony more. He would take her to the movies and kiss her on the neck. He would buy her dinner and ask her about work. He said he wanted to go somewhere far away. He said he wanted to be on her flight.

Arthur did a Halifax layover he was way too senior to fly, but he was trying to be home more. He was trying to try. Kathleen was in their backyard practising evacuation drills for her recurrent training. Recurrent training always happened at the beginning of May and it would always be just warm enough for her to do her studying outside.

"Emergency! Emergency! Keep your head down!" Kathleen yelled in the backyard. She could see Arthur watching from the back porch and he was still in his uniform. Kathleen was moving her arms, pointing to either side of the backyard like they were evacuation exits. Arthur was smiling and Kathleen could see the dimple in his left cheek.

"Arthur, what are you doing?"

"I like watching you do this. Remember when you would practise in our little place in Newfoundland and that one time our neighbour told you to shut the fuck up?" Arthur laughed, tossing his head back, and it made Kathleen miss him. She wondered if he had been with anyone else since Phoebe Klein and then she thought about Tony and how she hadn't mentioned him to Arthur, which she knew was against the rules.

"We should go to Hawaii," Arthur said. "We could take the boys. We haven't done it in years." Back at the start of their relationship they would bid their Hawaiis together.

"I don't know, Arthur."

"It'll be fun. The boys will love it."

"Arthur, c'mon, you're distracting me. I'm serious. This is an emergency."

Tony told her he loved her over a paper plane and Kathleen reminded him that she was married.

"I know, but you guys are seeing other people."

"Yes, in an effort to stay together."

"That doesn't make any sense."

"I know. I agree with you. It's confusing." Kathleen sipped her paper plane. "We're going to Hawaii next week."

"Who is?"

"Arthur and I, and the kids."

"Does he know about me?"

"No."

"Isn't that breaking the rules?"

Kathleen didn't know what the rules were anymore and she didn't know who was following them and who was breaking them. She was pretty certain that while she was protecting herself sexually she was not protecting herself personally and that people were going to get hurt. Kathleen had always wanted to follow the rules. She was a rule-follower and she was a pleaser. It was in her blood.

Arthur had cried after Kathleen told him about Tony. She had never seen him cry before and it made her feel things toward him that she never had. He had never stopped loving her and if he had, then he would have just left instead of coming up with games and rules and generating creative ways to fix things.

They met the boys down at the beach and Arthur walked a few feet in front of Kathleen the whole way there. They sat on towels as they watched people swim with the tide. When Ben and Andy came back to shore they built a sandcastle with the empty cup of a margarita Kathleen had just finished off in big gulps. Arthur wore sunglasses and read a magazine about flying. There was a plane on the front tilted sideways, which is something Arthur told the boys he had done in flight school. When he was done reading, he got up and put sunscreen on Ben's shoulders, rubbing it in until it disappeared. The boys put windows and doors on their sandcastle; they turned it into a beautiful home. Andy said he was tired and wanted to head back to the hotel. When Kathleen stood up she accidentally stepped on the side of the sandcastle, watching its walls fall down around her feet.

"Mom!" Ben yelled.

"Let's go," Andy said, slamming his bucket down and stomping away.

They all walked ten feet behind him back to the hotel with flip-flops dangling from their hands. Kathleen walked behind Arthur and she noticed that with his toe, he was drawing a line in the sand.

WINTER SALAD

"There should just be doctors and soldiers and farmers. The rest is just hocus-pocus," Sean said as he descended the stairs of the house they shared. "I don't know, actually, maybe we need firefighters too."

Jill had just finished her book and she bought black Adidas Sambas as a way of patting herself on the back. She had put Post-its of all her short stories on her wall and grouped them according to place and character and then put the groups in an order that she thought worked. Jill and Sean lived in the Annex with one other girl named Harper. Jill was finishing a master's in creative writing and worked part-time at Starbucks.

"So you're saying that everything I'm doing is useless?" Jill asked. But Sean was a writer too, so Jill mostly thought it was funny and laughed like if she was obsolete then so was he. Jill had known Sean since they were kids. Their parents went to the same Mommy and Me group in Guelph and they had drunk out of the same sippy cups from IKEA with the built-in straws.

"Did you hear about Simone?" Jill yelled because Sean was downstairs now.

"I heard she walked into oncoming traffic and she's in intensive care."

"Yeah. Isn't that fucked?" Jill said, and Sean popped his head into the stairs so he could see her. Then he nodded.

Jill's adviser was a well-known writer and critic. These days he was mostly publishing reviews in *Canadian Art* and *Toronto Life*. He was young and lucky. His name was Wayne Barry. Jill thought he was very charismatic for a man with two first names because she was of the opinion that those people were usually weird.

He was reviewing her full manuscript, which she had titled *Winter Salad*, and he told her to come to his office because he had notes. His office door was propped open with an anthology of Allen Ginsberg's poetry, which she thought was pretty tacky. She sat down in his office and stared out the huge window behind his desk. She could see the top of the CN Tower, but just barely, because it was foggy.

"Hey, you," Wayne said from behind her, touching Jill's shoulder. He was holding her manuscript in his hand, clutching it like a secret, and she noticed that his fingers were hairy in places.

"Hi," she said, and suddenly felt anxious looking at her thoughts on a stack of pages held together with a massive chip clip. "My parents used to have a chip clip like that," she said. "But we used it for like Doritos and stuff."

Wayne smiled at her and leaned his head on his hand. His hair had grown longer since the last time she had seen him and he had a beard. She had been in her room writing for weeks so they had only been corresponding on email. Sometimes he would sign off his emails with a winky face or a symbol for a heart which to her always looked like a penis.

"Jill, let me just say. You can get this published."

Jill felt her chest tighten and sighed. "I was hoping you would say that."

Wayne reached across his desk and put his hand over hers. "I'm proud of you."

"Thank you," Jill said. She heard footsteps outside his office and she moved her hand onto her lap.

"I want you to come to my fiction workshop Wednesday night at the downtown campus. I think it will be really nice and I want you to read from 'Dull Pencil.'"

"Dull Pencil" was a story Jill had written about her high school boyfriend. There was a scene where she lost her virginity that she absolutely never wanted her mother to read. "Okay, maybe," she said.

"No. I need you to. I'm trying to talk to my class about writing tasteful and accurate sex scenes. And I think you really nailed it here, Jill."

Jill thought about what Sean would say to Wayne. He would think Wayne was full of shit, someone who became successful too early. Sean would think that the world could use fewer Waynes.

Wayne Barry had been one of her favourite authors when she was younger. She had a distinct memory of her father taking her to Chapters when she was fourteen and buying Wayne's book. It was the first collection of short stories she read that made her feel like she could write. The cover of his book looked like the sky. It was beautiful. When she told her father Wayne was going to advise her graduate thesis, her father had read his book and told her she was lucky. But now Jill was older, she lived in a bigger city and she was sure that she and Wayne were really different people and really different writers. And she didn't know what he was doing to her.

Jill worked at Starbucks on Monday and Tuesday mornings. She would open while it was still dark and she would usually work bar. She would always open with the same girl, Sadie. Sadie was older than Jill and she only worked cash. She had a piercing on each nostril and she had a big blond streak in her hair. Sadie's girlfriend, Bea, would come get Sadie after work and sometimes the three of them would get a beer. On Saturday, during the weekend rush, while Jill was making a venti caramel macchiato, Sadie reached over and ran her hand over Jill's arm.

"How are you doing? You okay?"

Jill nodded and told Sadie she was fine even though she felt unstable.

Sadie clocked out a half-hour before Jill and waited for her out front while chain-smoking cigarettes. Jill sat down and ate a free tomato and mozzarella panini that had expired the day before.

"So what's your deal? You dating anyone?" Sadie asked when Jill sat down.

"No. I'm not. I live with this guy Sean and sometimes I think maybe that would be interesting, but I've known him forever so mostly I'm just like writing and slinging lattes." Jill could make anything serious into a joke. It helped her answer things she was uncomfortable with.

Sadie put her hand on Jill's leg. "You're a catch, you know that."

The next day Jill went to the dentist. Her insurance covered most of it so she only had to pay fifty dollars. The office had installed a television above the chair that hung down precariously above her head. The Oscars were that weekend and the news was anticipating the winners and the losers.

The hygienist, Betsy, asked Jill if she had a boyfriend. When Jill said she didn't, Betsy said, "Well that's okay, too."

Then Betsy asked Jill what she did for a living. Jill told her that she was a writer and she had just written a collection of short stories for her master's thesis. There was an instrument on her molar that made a humming sound.

"What are the stories about?" Betsy asked. She pulled the instrument out of Jill's mouth.

"I don't know, all sorts of things."

"You know, I think that's great. Because that's what stories should be! They should be about more than one thing. Like, you know, in the latest Nicholas Sparks novel, there's love but there's also suspense and there's even a murder in there!"

Jill nodded but she couldn't respond because Betsy was scraping the back of Jill's front teeth until they were clean.

"I knew that you were a creative type when you walked in," Betsy said.

A light was shining down onto Jill's face and making her tired. Jill always thought the reaction was funny when she told people she was a writer. Because they were a reader! Which meant there had to be a conversation.

"Do you like Nicholas Sparks?" Betsy asked.

"Yes," Jill said. "He's great." She smiled. Her teeth felt cleaner.

Betsy moved a bunch of instruments in Jill's mouth and then she took x-rays of her bite.

"I want to see what's really going on in there!" Betsy said. Jill looked down and noticed Betsy was wearing baby pink Puma shoes with her scrubs. "Honey, how tall are you!?" Betsy said as she put an x-ray vest around Jill's neck. Betsy told her she had just started seeing a guy who was six foot eight. "Do you have a boyfriend, sweetie?"

Jill wanted to tell her that they'd been over this but instead she stuck her chin in the x-ray machine and told her that she did.

She went to Wayne's class Wednesday night, like he asked, and she wore lipstick. She brought her story in her bag, printed out with extra spaces between lines so it was easier to read out loud. She had jotted some stuff in the margins and she felt excited to see Wayne. She took the subway to Osgoode and walked the rest of the way. It was April and it was starting to get warm.

"Hey," Wayne said when she walked into the seminar room. "Guys, this is Jill. She's finishing her thesis and I wanted her to come tonight to workshop one of her stories."

Jill tried to give him a look that would properly convey that that wasn't why she thought she was there.

"Jill, why don't you tell us a bit about yourself and your artist practice?"

She hated stuff like this but she agreed. "Hi, I'm Jill. I work at the Starbucks on Queen West and I just wrote a collection of short stories called *Winter Salad*. That title sounds ridiculous to me now that I'm saying it out loud." A few people laughed. "I don't know, I'm going to read a stupid thing I wrote called 'Dull Pencil.'"

Wayne was sitting beside her at the head of the table and

looked at her like he thought she was funny and important and it made Jill feel strange.

Before she read "Dull Pencil," they workshopped other students' stories. One kid who she had seen around campus read a story about dreaming that you roll over and kill your cat and wake up with a boner. Another girl, who Jill thought was beautiful, read a story about her boyfriend getting in a violent car accident and her finding out he was dead while she was eating fries with gravy. Jill pitched in and told them that the voice was confusing or she didn't think the reaction was right. Wayne looked at her the whole time and then told her it was her turn.

"Guys, I want you to pay attention to how Jill writes about sex."

She moved her foot slightly, coming in contact with Wayne's under the table. She quickly pulled her feet back so she was sitting cross-legged on her chair and started reading.

The scene about how she lost her virginity felt personal and weird to read to the class. She talked about how her high school boyfriend, Reid, had taken her to the drive-in and kissed her on piled blankets in his trunk, which was propped open so they could watch the animated movie *Cars*. Reid had been frustrated because it had taken Jill forever to want to have sex. But now he was seducing her slowly like that would help, and it did. He had moved his hand up her leg and he whispered in her ear that he thought she was beautiful. They had gone home after the drive-in and had sex on Reid's parents' couch in the basement and he had cum on a cushion that he washed with hand soap and just turned over, hoping no one would notice.

After she was done reading, Wayne led everyone in a

round of applause. "Now, let's workshop 'Dull Pencil,'" he said.

"Oh, I don't need to take up your time with that."

"No, Jill." Wayne put his hand on her arm. "We're going to workshop the story."

The guy with the cat and boner story said that he didn't think it sounded real. "It doesn't sound real. Like her giving him a hand job during *Cars*. Would that actually happen?"

Jill thought about how it did happen and then she felt embarrassed.

"Yeah, and like this Marcy character, she seems like a bitch," another guy said. "And like why would she wait so long to have sex with her boyfriend?"

"Yeah, I could do without that character," a girl said from the other end of the table before Jill could respond.

"Sorry, you could do without the main character?" Jill asked, confused. The class didn't seem to be picking up on how this was essentially her.

Wayne looked at her. "All right Jill, well, you've got some things to consider."

"I mean I can't cut the protagonist from the story, Wayne."

"Hey, don't get defensive. We're just giving you ideas for how to enhance the work."

Jill resented how Wayne had manipulated her into coming to read for his class by framing it like an opportunity. She resented that writing workshops sometimes required smiling while people wrote stories you hated and asked for asinine details about what kind of shampoo the protagonist used. Jill smiled and thanked Wayne for the help.

Jill didn't have many friends in the city, so after the workshop she texted Sadie and asked her to go for a beer. Sadie met her at a bar in Kensington Market with taps on the wall and a good patio. Jill told her about Wayne and how she thought he was fucking with her.

"I don't know. It's really weird to have someone who you really respect reading your work because they can like get inside your head, you know." Jill took a massive sip from an IPA brewed in Muskoka, near her parents' cottage.

Sadie put her hand on Jill's hand and told her she was amazing and she was a good writer and she didn't need this guy to validate her.

"But I do need him to validate me! He like helps decide if I graduate and get this collection published." Jill paused and looked at Sadie. She liked how much Sadie liked her but there was something strange about her. It felt like Sadie was observing her—collecting information for later. "And you know what else is crazy?" Jill sipped her beer. "This girl I know from back home like walked into traffic last week and now she's dead."

"Maybe you should write about that."

"Oh my God. You're so right. I should." Jill thought about how she probably shouldn't, but she thought Wayne would love it and that made her want to use it.

Sadie asked Jill about her past relationships. She told Sadie about Reid and how she'd thought she was in love when she was very young. "He was a really good guy but I didn't really feel like myself when I lived in Guelph. I don't know, I think I want different things now. I want to write and feel successful professionally and creatively and I'm not as concerned with personal relationships."

Sadie nodded and started talking about Bea and how it was their one-year anniversary in a few days and Sadie just wasn't sure how to feel. She talked about how she didn't think Bea was very funny and how they had pretty normal sex and Sadie just wanted different things. Sadie bought Jill another beer and said, "Don't worry, it's on me."

When Jill got home she wrote the story about the girl walking into traffic. She thought the dialogue between the parents was really strong and she thought with some editing, it would be ready for a whole handful of lit journals. She hoped that Simone's parents didn't read it because it was fiction! And it was only loosely based on their daughter.

She woke up with a splitting headache and emailed the story to Wayne. He told her to meet him at his office that afternoon. When she arrived he told her to take a seat on his couch. He sat down and angled himself toward her with his arm slung over the back of the couch. He took out a copy of her story that he had printed and stapled at the top. There was a lot of red pen on the page and Wayne said, "Don't worry, it's really brilliant." He went page by page telling her his favourite parts. "And the part in the traffic. I mean, I think it's amazing that you start naming the brands of the cars before they hit her. It really prolongs the grief and then when it happens you just feel it hit you all at once, like a car."

"I'm really glad you like it," Jill said. "You know, I felt weird about writing it at first because it's just this like really fresh thing that happened in my hometown but—I—"

When Wayne kissed her she felt the leather of the couch. It felt like an animal underneath her. She was sweating and she was worried that when she got up the leather would be wet. Wayne grabbed her hip while he kissed her and she felt like his handprint would be there later. He pulled away and walked back behind his desk. He picked up a green and yellow stress ball on his desk and squeezed it until the veins in his arm popped out.

"You're a very talented writer, Jill."

When Jill got home she told Sean what happened and he dropped the mug he was holding and when it hit the floor only the handle came off.

"That is not okay," Sean said. He was still finishing courses and was jealous of Jill being able to write all the time.

"I don't know. I showed him this story I wrote about Simone walking into traffic, and he really liked it and I don't know, it was confusing. He's validating all my thoughts. It's like he knows me."

"That's sexual harassment, he's not allowed to do that," Sean said. He was standing in the kitchen, separated from her by an island that held all their spices on a rack that spun clockwise. "And why are you even writing about Simone? That's not your story to tell. Did you even know the funeral is like this weekend?" He threw the whole mug in the garbage and Jill thought to herself that she would only have thrown out the handle. "I think I'm going to go home for the funeral." Sean looked at Jill like he was disappointed and sad for her. He told her that she was strong and her work was important and she didn't need to kiss Wayne Barry to feel like all that was true. Then he told her she needed to be smarter.

When Jill got to work the next day, Sadie didn't speak to her the whole morning. At lunch, Jill drank a bottled smoothie from the work cooler and paid six dollars for it. Sadie came into the back room and took off her green apron, throwing it on the milk order.

"Hey, is something wrong?" Jill asked.

"Do you think that you're gay?"

"Excuse me?"

"I think you might be gay."

"Well, you don't really know me."

"I have a crush on you."

"Sadie, that's nice, but I'm not interested." Jill's apron suddenly felt tight on the back of her neck, like it was pulling.

"I'm going to break up with Bea."

"Don't do that. You guys seem great together."

"Well, I have feelings for you!"

"I don't know what to say, Sadie. I'm sorry." Jill chugged the end of her smoothie and the last sip tasted like celery. She went back to the floor and punched in early on the till. There was a line out the door and she hopped back on the bar. She drizzled a caramel macchiato with her right hand as she stopped a shot of espresso with her left. She called drinks out at the bar. "Extra hot, no foam, skinny vanilla latte." She was good at this. This is something she could manage, even though it was complicated.

That night Jill's phone lit up every ten minutes while she slept. It was Sadie calling her a bitch and saying that she didn't care about people. It was Sadie saying that she needed to confront her sexuality and stop being seduced by her teacher. And then it was Sean saying that he was sorry and she should come to his room so he could apologize. She stood in his doorway in her pyjamas and when he looked up she climbed into his bed.

"It's not your fault. I'm sorry. I shouldn't have blamed you. But you need to tell someone about this. What he did is not okay."

"Sadie told me she has a crush on me."

"What?"

"Look at these messages."

"Holy shit," Sean said. "What are you going to do?"

"I think I'm going to have to transfer. Or quit."

"You can't quit."

Jill blocked Sadie's number the next day. She talked to her shift supervisor, who laughed and then realized she was serious. He transferred her to the store at the Eaton Centre, which was really just a booth outside Victoria's Secret and Jill thanked him with a hug. Jill took the Greyhound with Sean to Guelph that Saturday and went to Simone's funeral. A lot of people from her high school were there and they all looked pretty and healthy. Jill had dinner in her parents' newly renovated kitchen and told them everything in her life was on track. Her parents asked her questions about Wayne's influence and Jill told them his influence was powerful and her father smiled like it was a good thing. Jill and Sean walked downtown and drank six beers in the parking lot of Church of Our Lady. The church was so tall you could see it from everywhere in the city, or that's what people said anyway. When Jill got back to Toronto she dragged the story about Simone walking into traffic into the trash can on her desktop, then she cleared the garbage so she could hear the sound of paper shredding.

FLAT CIRCLE

Charlotte's parents started getting into weed right after her dad's first heart attack. They called every Sunday at noon like clockwork, but this call was different. They were humming and hawing and forgetting what they were about to say.

"What's wrong with you guys?"

"Honey, we're high as kites."

Earlier that winter, Charlotte's dad had had a heart attack while shovelling their driveway. The statistics of that happening were high. It was common! Probable, even! When Charlotte got to her dad's hospital room she told him that. It was a tale as old as time: men are prone to heart attacks while shovelling. She hit him on the arm when she said this, but then she felt bad, so she started rubbing his shoulder with such apologetic vigour that she wondered if that was also hurting him. Charlotte wasn't surprised by this turn of events in her father's health because she'd always thought of him as kind of weak. Not in a bad way: he was just sensitive and lovely and his lip quivered at the drop of a hat.

Charlotte went to Memorial University, where she was paying an arm and a leg to get an undergraduate degree in social work. She worked at a Shoppers Drug Mart down the street from her residence and lately they'd been sticking her in the cosmetics section. Her boss, Lucy, dyed a streak of her hair a different colour every week in accordance with her mood. Lucy encouraged Charlotte to take an hour after lunch to walk up and down the nail polish aisle and roll each polish between her hands until she could hear the little ball hitting the sides of the bottle with a clink.

"We got to keep 'em fresh, you know." Lucy was fixing her hair in a small mirror beside the condoms and tampons. "'Cause you knows the polish will all start stickin' together and then we've gotta get a whole new stock."

Charlotte nodded like she understood, so every day at noon she would walk back to her residence, rip a bong, and come back for the nail polish. If Charlotte took any time at all to think about the banality of the task, she would spiral, so instead she thought about Jack, a boy from her Neo-liberal Novel class who she had started hanging out with. Jack was simple but also complicated in a way that reminded her of her father. His hair was long and he parted it in the middle and he tucked it behind his ears whenever he made an authoritative point in class. He played bass in a band called Flat Circle and they toured Eastern Canada every summer and came back with half the money they left with.

Jack had a girlfriend named JD, who apparently loved Salinger. Both Jack and JD went to MUN and Charlotte would see them together, chewing the ends of their pens in the Queen Elizabeth II Library. JD's hair was blond and cut in blunt chunks that framed her face. She had tiny silver and gold earrings in three different spots on her ears and Charlotte couldn't stop looking at her. Charlotte also wondered what JD stood for, thinking the initials were a trick that added to her mystery.

Charlotte and Jack were partners in a study group where they had to read Tom Wolfe's *Bonfire of the Vanities* and talk about the implications of the guilt that weighed on each character. After they analyzed the last chapter, Jack kissed Charlotte on the mouth and it made her feel high. Charlotte told him that what they were doing was wrong and that the guilt would eat her up like the people in the book and Jack kissed her ear and asked what they should do.

A week later, Jack came over to watch TV; he had a bag of Orville Redenbacher popcorn swinging from his hand. It just sat on the counter, though, when Charlotte told him she didn't have a microwave. They sat on the small pink couch in her residence and watched *True Detective*. Jack started playing with her hair with his left hand while he drank a craft beer with the right.

"Okay, this part is the best," Jack said, moving his hand down to her neck.

A very dishevelled-looking Matthew McConaughey was talking about life and the nature of relationships and at one point he said, "Time is a flat circle."

"What does that mean?" Charlotte asked.

"It means that the things we do, we're going to do them over and over and over again. We're doomed to repeat patterns."

She kissed Jack on the lips and went to her room and grabbed a preroll she'd bought from the weed store on Water Street.

Jack paused the TV and they lit the joint and stared at the ceiling.

"You know, my parents are getting into weed," Charlotte said.

"It's going to be legal next Tuesday," Jack replied. "My parents are like crazy Conservatives and they think everyone's gonna lose their mind."

"I think I've lost mine," Charlotte said.

She looked at Jack as he laughed and inhaled the weed, holding it in his lungs for what seemed like forever. She thought then that this person might break her.

Charlotte's mom, lately, was in the habit of building things. First it was stools for the backyard table and then it was a wine rack. Recently, she'd been trying her hand at a bedside table for Charlotte's old room. Charlotte promised her mother that she would not be moving home and therefore would not be drinking beverages in bed, but her mother didn't listen. The problem with the things her mother built was that they broke, easily. A little bit of weight and the whole thing crashed down around you. As opposed to this being annoying, Charlotte had begun to think of it as endearing. She started to realize and appreciate the helplessness of her parents and the relationship they had to the world.

Weed became legal the next week and there was a party on George Street. The weed store on Water Street sold out and there was a line wrapped around the building like a membrane. Charlotte and Jack went to the party and held hands in line. They smoked from a small, warm joint Jack had stuffed in his pocket. Charlotte was looking over her shoulder the whole time since engaging in anything dishonest in St. John's was always a terrible idea because everyone knew everyone.

"Where's JD?"

"She's visiting her parents in Toronto," Jack said. He was avoiding Charlotte's eyes and she knew it was because he felt guilty.

Charlotte thought of her first boyfriend, Luke, as she stared at Jack bathed in the blue light of the club's sign. Luke was a huge pothead, and whenever he smoked Charlotte said she wasn't interested. When he moved away after high school to go to McGill, Charlotte cried every day for a month and then bought her bong. Now her anxiety could only be managed with weed. She carried a little pipe with smiley faces on it in her back pocket and she smoked whenever she felt like things were too heavy. She looked behind her in line at all the people celebrating legal weed and she wondered if they were feeling heavy too.

When she went over for family dinner that Sunday, Charlotte's mom asked her to roll a joint. So while the chicken was roasting, Charlotte brought her weed to the dinner table.

"We went to that new legal weed store downtown! It's like an Apple store in there, baby," her dad yelled from the next room, where he was watching CNN.

"Yeah, did you hear they ran out though?" Charlotte yelled, as she concentrated on keeping the joint tight. "No one can get weed right now. There's a countrywide shortage."

"People are so greedy, honey," her dad yelled. "No one knows how to share!"

Jack picked Charlotte up from her residence at the university that night and told her he wanted a green thumb. He couldn't afford anything at Holland Nurseries though, so they went to the Delta at 10 p.m. and took clippings from every plant in the lobby. Charlotte laughed and stuffed the clippings in the pocket of her raincoat until she looked suspicious.

When they got back into Jack's parents' Mazda they unloaded their pockets and filled the cupholders with the plant clippings.

"I think I might try to get my hands on a weed plant. It might be fun to see if I can grow it."

Charlotte thought he was cute when he had a plan. "What are you doing tonight? Do you want to come over?" she asked.

"I have to go to JD's place. Her parents are in town for the weekend so I've gotta show face, you know. Even though I would rather kill myself." He looked at her from the driver's seat and his face was backlit from a car that was parked behind him.

Jack made comments about killing himself too haphazardly. It was like a social crutch he could lean on to add an element of danger to the conversation.

"I'm gonna break up with her, you know."

"I mean, don't do anything you don't want to do," Charlotte said, feeling weak and unsure about what she wanted and like she didn't know how to adequately reply to a lot of the things Jack said. She didn't know if this was her fault or if he was making things harder for her.

"No, I know what I have to do," he said, tucking his hair

behind his ear. Somehow whenever he did this, it convinced her to believe him.

Jack started the car and it struggled a bit so she knew he'd forgotten to get gas. Charlotte looked at her Instagram as Jack drove out of the Delta parking lot. Her childhood friend Rachel had uploaded ten stories where she talked into the camera about her ex-boyfriend and how badly he'd treated her. Charlotte pointed the phone at Jack as the car slowly sputtered up Flower Hill and together they watched Rachel's breakdown on social media.

"This is crazy," Jack said. "Like it sounds like they had a bad breakup. Does that mean he's an abuser?"

"I haven't talked to this person since like high school and now I have intimate information about her life that I would never otherwise know."

Jack dropped Charlotte off at her residence and she touched his knee before she left the car. She went inside and ripped a bong and lay in her bed until her eyes started to close.

Jack never did break up with JD and Charlotte never told him that the way he made her feel was weird and scary. But the next month she saw him on the steps of the Ship with another girl and she thought about time being a flat circle.

She pulled out her phone once to Instagram a story about how she felt played and hurt by this person but she closed it without uploading. She did feel a certain power, though, and like maybe everyone everywhere could connect about their pain and maybe it all wasn't as crazy as she thought.

The semester ended and Charlotte used her school health insurance to go to a student dentist. While standing over her, cleaning her teeth, the hygienist asked her if she smoked cigarettes.

"No, but I smoke a lot of weed."

"You should stop doing that, you have holes in your teeth."

Charlotte wanted to tell him that she had holes in her brain too, which is why she couldn't stop.

SWIFFER WETJET

When the dog died, they got Big Macs. They sat in the parking lot with their car running and ate out of brown bags with greasy bottoms that made their legs wet. Noah reached his hand over and covered Bridget's knee.

"He was a good dog," Noah said and Bridget could see the meat in his mouth tossed around and around like clothes in a dryer. He couldn't seem to swallow.

"He was." When Bridget said this, she started crying so when she swallowed, she choked. The heat from the car was shooting at both her face and her ankles and making her hot. She tried to open the car door but it was locked. She was breathing heavily and Noah's hand was still on her leg.

"I'm going to get you a drink," he said, getting out of the car. "That will make you feel better." He sounded so far away they could have been separated by an ocean. When he came back with the drink, she noticed that his hair was getting more grey by the ears and down by the neck.

"It's hard to think about our life without him."

"It's impossible."

Noah kissed her shoulder, which felt like something he had never done before. He kept his mouth there and rested his forehead against her ear. "I hope we're not lost."

They drove up to Queen East. Bridget kept the heat off and told Noah to take Kingston Road. "What? It's faster," she said, when he looked at her sideways.

When they walked into the house, there was a silence so sad it was crushing. Bridget thought about it just being her and Noah now, and how the dog had kept them from having conversations they should have had about commitments they should have made. Noah walked toward the bathroom undoing his belt. She heard the shower running seconds later and she felt thankful for the noise.

Noah worked for an advertising agency called ReImagine. He had been reimagining for twenty-one years this June. There was something funny about having people work so long at a job where things are always supposed to be new. Noah would come home and tell her stories about how twenty-two-year-olds were now sitting in on their meetings. They were crossing their legs the same way as Noah and chewing on the end of their pens with new and exciting vigour, the way he used to.

After the dog died, Noah lost his joie de vivre. Or at least that's what his boss said. He pulled Noah into his office and said he needed to get creative and start thinking of new ideas. Things that were fresh! They were in charge of promoting a new Labatt beer, brewed in Newfoundland, and they wanted Noah to be their point person. They gave him a blue binder and told him not to fuck it up.

When Noah got home he kissed Bridget on her forehead

in the same place as always and said, "Let's go to Newfoundland."

"Why would we do that?"

"I have to promote this new beer and it's brewed there and I've never been!"

"Noah, I don't think they meant you have to go to Newfoundland. Just think of some ideas." Bridget was making a lasagne for dinner, adding new layers with precision. "Plus, we can't afford it right now anyway. You know that." They had just paid a fortune in veterinary bills and they had still lost something profound.

"Lasagne?" Noah asked, changing the subject. They lived in a small bungalow with beige walls. The living room was attached to the kitchen and Noah always turned on the TV when he got home, crossing his feet on the coffee table as she made dinner. They always had lasagne on Thursdays but Bridget hoped this went unnoticed. Noah turned the TV up louder than normal and she thought it was because there was no dog.

"See, look at this commercial! Everything is big, it's new, it's fresh."

"So? You can do that!" Bridget said.

"Yeah, but am I just going to do what everyone else is doing? I need to move away from the obvious. I need something shocking."

Bridget looked at Noah's eyes and for a second she thought he looked manic. She looked back at the lasagne, six layers, getting worse as they went. She slid it into the oven and waited.

Bridget was a high school teacher. She taught at Malvern, which was only seconds from their house in the Beaches. Every morning, she would take the dog for a walk before she came back and made herself a salad with spinach, chick peas and olive oil and pack it in a long, thin glass Tupperware.

That day at work, one of her students, Alicia, booked an appointment with her after school and told her she was pregnant. Her boyfriend had come inside her and she didn't know what to do. She hadn't had forty dollars at the time for the Plan B pill and now she needed an abortion. Alicia was a good one. And she didn't know how good, which was an important thing about her. Bridget knew Alicia's parents from the neighbourhood and she remembered Alicia's small pink bike with the training wheels from years ago.

"Honey, you have options," Bridget said and Alicia started crying. Bridget wanted to take her out for a Big Mac and explain loss like she knew something. Bridget was suddenly angry at this boy who got Alicia pregnant. She was mad that he didn't pull out and didn't follow up. She was mad that he didn't kiss her on the shoulder and buy her a root beer.

The dog's name was Swiffer. When he was a puppy they had spent weeks on a name. Noah had been fascinated with the new Swiffer technology right before the millennium, and he couldn't believe he hadn't thought of it first. So he took the name for the dog because he wanted it to mean something different and stop reminding him of his shortcomings.

"It's a broom that shoots water. Isn't that amazing!" Noah said as he held the Swiffer toward her like a shotgun.

Bridget came home from work and Noah was home first, which almost never happened. He was sitting at the kitchen table, clicking a pen in perfect rhythm. After Bridget toed off her shoes she came up behind him and looked at the list he was writing. It had three three-letter, bullet-point words on it: New, Big, Wet. Bridget chuckled and put her hand on his shoulder when she passed him. Bridget had stopped getting her period that year. First there was some spotting and then there was nothing. She would wake up in the middle of the night with sweat running down her cheeks. She would tiptoe to the washroom down the hall, stepping on the floorboards she knew didn't make noise.

That night when she got back to bed, Noah's eyes were open. She lay down beside him and turned to her side so she couldn't see him. "Why didn't we ever have kids?" she asked quietly.

"You didn't want them," Noah said back immediately like he had known why all along.

It was so quiet Bridget could hear the clicks of Noah's watch, which he never took off.

"Do you think that was a mistake?" she asked as Noah's hand on her waist began to feel heavy.

"Why are you thinking about this?"

"One of my students is pregnant and she wants an abortion," she said. Noah hummed like he was sorry and Bridget thought about how she loved him. "And our dog is dead."

"Do you want to have a kid?"

Bridget laughed hard and turned around so she was facing him. "I'm old and small and dried up." *New, Big, Wet.*

Noah kissed her when she said this and it made her want to kiss him on the eyelids and tell him he was perfect. She rolled on top of him, which was how they always had sex. Noah took her tank top off and she felt cold with dried sweat. His hands felt so familiar like it was her own skin. She knew where his hands were lined on the palms. He put his hand on her breast and said, "Baby."

"What?" Bridget put his hand on her stomach and she felt his body still.

"I think something's—I—"

"What?"

"I can feel a lump. There." He put pressure on her breast with his thumb like he was having a thumb war. "Here, feel it."

Bridget turned the light on and she told him to stop it. She thought about Alicia and she thought about the dog. She kept her hand on her chest all night and dreamed of being on cruise ships with waves coming over top of her, soaking her to the bone. She woke up in a sweat and Noah had left a note on the bed telling her he'd called the doctor and had gone to the office to brainstorm how to sell things.

Bridget hadn't had a mammogram in two years and she was kicking herself. She took the week off work and she thought about Alicia and who would be there for her. One day she even made the spinach salad with chick peas and olive oil and put it in the fridge after she realized she wasn't going to work. Noah met her downtown near his office for an appointment with their doctor, who had more hair in his ears than she remembered. He told her that her cancer was treatable but she might want to consider a mastectomy. "You know, breast cancer is more common in women who decide not to have children."

This made Bridget's breath hitch in her throat.

"Dr. Harris, we just lost our dog," Noah said.

"I'm sorry to hear that. However, you're going to have to think about your options." He handed them a binder that was the same blue as the one Noah's boss had given him for the Labatt deal. "I usually recommend that you go see our grief specialist. Her name is Missy and her office is on the first floor. Something like this can be very traumatic when you don't see it coming."

They booked an appointment with Missy for the end of the week. Her office was an inoffensive green and she had lots of plants to match. When Missy asked Noah how he was feeling about everything he went on a long tirade about how everything in their lives had been the same for so long and he felt almost crippled by having to confront serious things he didn't anticipate. He talked about advertising and how it was his job to create new and meaningful reasons for people to buy things they don't already have, but how it was getting harder the more it became clear that he had everything he was ever going to have.

Bridget responded by saying that she wasn't sure Noah cared about her feelings all the time and also that she felt he had always resented her for not giving him kids. She said she was tired of always being on top and how she longed for the past when her breasts were full and without lumps and when she would have to use super tampons for at least the first two days of a period. She said that she felt she and Noah knew each other too well and they suffered from an overwhelming and intimate knowledge of how the other thought.

Missy said that it was normal for them both to long for

things past and she charged them three hundred dollars for the hour.

"I feel like I was just mugged," Noah said when they left the building. They were spit onto Yonge Street out of revolving doors.

"Did you know this is the longest road in Canada?" Bridget said.

"What, Yonge?"

That night Bridget found a letter from Alicia in their mailbox. She was having the abortion in two days and she wanted Bridget there.

Bridget picked Alicia up at the school two days later and when Alicia got in the front seat Bridget spent a minute looking at her face. "You know, I used to watch you ride your bike with the training wheels. I remember the day your dad took them off."

"Really?"

Bridget stopped at a red light. "Yeah, I looked out my front window and your little helmet was falling off the back of your head. I would only push my curtains aside a little bit though so you wouldn't see me."

Alicia looked scared but also comforted and her hands were under her legs.

"It was the only time I thought I may want children," Bridget said. She pulled the car over and hit the curb. "Are you sure you want to do this, honey?"

Alicia nodded her head and bit on her bottom lip until it started to bleed.

"I'm sure," she said.

Bridget felt proud of her certainty.

Afterwards, Bridget drove them back to her house and Alicia came inside for a chamomile tea. She put her hands on either side of the mug and shivered. Bridget turned on the TV and it made her feel better. She patted the spot on the couch beside her twice and Alicia sat down. They squeezed under the same blanket and Bridget said, "I think you're strong. You remind me of me."

There was a late daytime episode of *Days of Our Lives* playing that Bridget knew because she had become acquainted with the realities of daytime television this past week.

"Why are you taking time off school?" Alicia asked.

"Oh, just some things in my life are changing."

The television switched to commercials. The first commercial was for Molson, Noah's competition. It started in the living room of a married couple with no children, drinking beer from the fridge. A woman with a silky voice said, "Have a drink that fits your new normal," and the commercial flashed back to the couple. They had no kids and they were eating a lasagne. It was hard to tell on screen, but Bridget thought the layers looked like they got worse as they went.

HALFWAY SOMEWHERE

Frank and I broke up at the AGO, the day after Valentine's. Toronto was slushy and dreary and I didn't feel good. We had taken a Megabus from Kingston, where we both went to school, and we stayed at Frank's parents' house in the Beaches. Frank's father was reading *The Odyssey* and I told him I had never seen anyone over twenty-five read it. Frank's mother had made a bed for me in the basement and put a mint on the pillow. I ate the mint as I was trying to fall asleep and sent Frank a text saying, "what's up?"

His parents both worked at Toronto Metropolitan University and they took the subway to work holding hands. They were both disciplined and concerned and as I stared at them over the Valentine's stew, I honestly thought they could have been twins. The stew had been in the slow cooker since the morning and Frank's mother said to me, "Roxane, I hope you like carrots."

I remember nodding and moaning very loudly, indicating I loved carrots. Frank's father looked at me from the end of the table, with his head tilted to the left. "So, you like Homer?"

I asked, folding the beige napkin on my lap in a triangle.

"Simpson?" his mother said. She was scooping the stew onto plates edged with yellow flowers. As she was handing a full plate to Frank it tipped and fell like an avalanche into brown layers on her white tablecloth. In my memory she said something like, "Oh, goodness me," and the pile of stew was left there as we began to eat. Then Frank's father grabbed my hand and I jumped until my knees hit the table.

"We have to pray, Roxane," Frank's father announced loudly like a command.

My family always prayed before dinner too. We hardly ever held hands because everyone was always too hungry.

"Oh, hold on, I just need to light the candles," Frank's mother said, jumping from the table and running on her tippy toes to the kitchen. I was still holding Frank's father's hand and for a second it felt wrong. I could feel my hands getting sweaty and I tried to catch Frank's eye across from me, but he was staring at the pile of stew left on the table like a dead animal. Once the candles were lit, the room started to smell of lavender, which I was allergic to. Frank's mother sat down and grabbed my other hand, the one that was not holding her husband's. Frank's father said the prayer. He talked about Valentine's Day and how much he loved his wife. I thought they would be looking at each other but everyone's eyes were closed, their heads bowed almost ninety degrees. I kept my eyes open and looked between Frank's mother and father. I could have sworn they were related. Later I wanted to tell Frank this, but thought it was better to not.

"Amen," everyone except me said when the prayer was finished.

Frank's parents asked me all the regular questions over

dinner and I answered with stew in my mouth. "Yes, I like Queen's . . . I want to be a writer, maybe . . . My parents still live in Waterloo . . . I have a half-brother, but we didn't grow up together."

The cat, whose name was Jennifer, hopped onto the table and started eating the stew off the tablecloth. I wondered if that was the intention the whole time. No one seemed disturbed or even inclined to acknowledge her.

"We only had Frankie here, but we tried for another one, that's for sure. Didn't we, honey?"

Their incessant optimism was giving me a headache and I could feel myself smiling more frequently than I ever would normally. I watched Frank eat his meal in heaping spoonfuls, not acknowledging his parents' conversation at all. He had tucked his beige napkin halfway down his shirt and he was doing things his way.

That night, Frank's mother gave him the keys to the car and told him to be home in ninety minutes.

"Why wouldn't she just say an hour and a half?" I asked him as I jumped down his parents' porch steps two at a time.

"I don't know. Don't ask me. I don't understand half of what comes out of their mouths."

"I didn't know that."

"You didn't know what?"

"That they were like that."

"I don't know what you mean."

I was starting to realize Frank was the type of person who was not okay with anyone insulting his parents while he simultaneously treated them like shit.

"Never mind," I said, and I grabbed his hand.

"Your hand is all sweaty."

"Oh yeah, it's from the prayer."

I thought he was anxious but I didn't push it.

We drove to a Scarborough Dairy Queen in his mom's old car they kept in the garage. I told him a story about how my brother had come to my ninth birthday party and thrown a pie in my face.

"What? Why?"

"It was part of the joke. You would like spin a wheel or whatever and one of the options was a pie in the face."

"Why would anybody want that?"

"Because you got to lick it off after." I paused. "But I remember it being funny because I remember this woman who worked at the restaurant was going to do it and then at the last second my brother took the pie from her hand. It almost felt like a punishment, but I didn't know why he was punishing me."

Frank furrowed his brow like he didn't know where this story was going, which is something that happened with us often.

"I don't know. Everyone laughed and so I laughed too 'cause I was nine. But it upset me."

"Yeah?" Frank asked. "Did you tell him that?"

"No. I just licked the pie off my face."

Frank found a tape in the glove compartment that said SUMMER JAMS on it. There was a sun with a smiley face drawn in thick Sharpie and it made me feel closer to Frank. He got excited and told me he'd made this tape when he was in middle school and it would be funny to listen to, like a blast from the past. When he put it on, though, it played a Bach concerto. Someone had recorded over his summer jams. I didn't know which concerto it was, but I had a memory of my parents playing it and slow dancing in our living room after my dad retired. Frank got really mad about the tape and cracked it in two, chucking it out the window like a frisbee.

"They just can't let anything be mine." His face was red and he ran a red light but I didn't say anything. Frank could get really mad on a dime. It was never directed at me but each time I found it incredibly off-putting.

Frank used his father's MasterCard to buy me a Blizzard at the Dairy Queen. They were featuring a special love Blizzard that was larger than normal. A guy whose name tag said BART stuck two spoons inside, tipped it upside down, which is something I never understood, and handed it to us like it was a new baby.

"Enjoy," he said.

"Why do they always tip it upside down?" I asked Frank as I leaned in toward his shoulder.

"We have to make sure it stays together!" BART said. "We don't want any falling out." He leaned toward us over the counter. "Plus, I think it looks kinda cool."

Frank told me as we walked out that it was an advertising campaign from 2015 and he was surprised I didn't remember. When we got outside, Frank took the first bite, which didn't surprise me. It had started raining and I noticed Frank's red spoon was still in his mouth. He was wearing a red wool Filson coat that he'd found at the Value Village the previous summer. He took it off and handed it to me, insisting I put it on. "I think we're supposed to get a blizzard," he said.

We ran to the car and Frank fell on his back. I turned around and laughed and immediately felt bad so I threw my hand over my mouth and bent down to where he was lying. I moved his dark hair off his forehead.

"Are you okay?"

"I heard a crack."

"I think that was thunder," I told him and I think he was hurt that I didn't just agree.

He limped to the car and before he opened the door, he told me he wanted to have sex.

I agreed and we got into the back seat. The Mercedes was perfect and the seats shone. I said, "Should we do this here? I feel bad about the car."

"It's fine, Roxane. It's Valentine's."

I put the half-eaten Blizzard on the floor of the car and asked Frank if he was up for this after falling.

"Turn around," he said. So I took my pants off and slid around on the perfect seats of his mom's old car, thinking about the prayer at dinner.

"I think your parents really love each other," I told him when I was facing the other way, toward the window. I thought about how my parents used to put our dogs in the back seat of our RAV4 so we could drive to the dog park. The dogs always hated the drive.

He didn't answer and it was a minute before he said, "Shit, I can't get hard."

The windows were foggy and I felt hot. My knees were sticking to the leather seat and I thought about how I would have rather been looking at him while we had sex on Valentine's. I closed my eyes and breathed deep and could hear him grunting behind me in a way that made me wonder if he really needed me at all.

"Hold on a sec," he whispered and grabbed my ass in a

disconnected way like it was a door knob or something.

Then I saw, out the passenger window, BART from the Dairy Queen. He was wearing a blue uniform polo shirt with a little ice cream cone in the corner. His visor was wet and there was water falling off the brim. His eyes met mine from where he stood a few feet away and I suddenly felt embarrassed.

"Fuck it," Frank said.

I looked back and saw that he was only halfway hard.

"It's just not working."

I pulled up my pants and looked down at the floor. The Valentine's Blizzard had spilt all over the back of the car. It was white and creamy and the two spoons were sitting in either side of the puddle.

Frank's parents had a membership to the Art Gallery of Ontario and they told us to enjoy. So the next day we took the streetcar along Dundas and Frank sat down while I stood up.

"I don't even know this guy."

"Well, he's dead."

"Who?"

"The painter. Alex Colville." The streetcar stopped and I lost my footing and fell into a girl wearing a Canada Goose jacket. I remembered my mother telling me about Alex Colville. She had a coffee-table book at our house in Waterloo and on the front there was a woman staring at you with binoculars. "I remember finding his paintings of women really interesting when I was younger," I told Frank.

The thing about Frank was he was aesthetically out of touch. It limited our ability to talk about things I considered beautiful or important.

"How's your back today?"

"It's bruised a bit, but it's fine," he said. His eyes were sunken and dark like they were bruised.

When we got to the AGO, they offered to give us headsets. We both put them on so we couldn't hear each other. When we walked into the gallery they were screening a scene from a Wes Anderson movie, *Moonrise Kingdom*. Frank lifted the headset and held it above his head about two inches. "That girl kind of looks like you."

It was clear he'd never seen the movie but I smiled and appreciated Frank for being observant and nice when I didn't expect him to. We walked through the gallery like it was a maze. I paused in front of a painting I recognized from my mom's book. In the painting, a mother was putting her two young kids in a car, a boy and a girl.

"I like this one," I said, leaning over toward Frank.

"What?"

"Never mind," I said. I pulled the headphones off and they dropped to the floor and the string hung from my pocket like a leash. I looked around at the paintings and felt happy for Alex Colville and his wife. I really believed that they had found something special with each other. "I think we should break up," I said to Frank quietly like I wasn't sure.

"What?" Frank said.

"I think we should break up," I said louder this time.

"I was just getting to the good part!" he said loudly, pointing to the headphones.

"I'm gonna go!" I yelled. I looked toward the gift shop. There was a mother pointing at the door. Her head was covering the A of AGO. GO, it said, like a sign that I should run. "I'm gonna go!" I yelled again louder and my palms turned toward the sky like I was frustrated or like I was praying maybe. Frank didn't seem to notice and if he did, he didn't say anything.

I took the streetcar down Queen and back to Frank's parents' house. His mother let me in and I told her something about Frank running into a friend and staying downtown. I told her he loved the exhibit and that he thought it was an interesting comment on women.

After getting my things, I took an early bus back to Kingston and kept my head against the window the whole time. My brother was picking me up the next Friday to go to our dad's house in Waterloo and I thought about how I would avoid seeing Frank until then.

2/2

After nearly an hour on the road, my brother asks me if I believe in God. Instead of answering him, I pretend I'm asleep, with my mouth open on the closed window. I can imagine him rolling his eyes but I don't look to confirm because I am pretending to be asleep.

My half-brother Tyler lives in the Ottawa Valley. He's recently met a girl online and she works for the government. He sometimes visits her at Parliament even though he's a socialist and thinks Trudeau is a hack. I wonder if this makes things hard for them, not having the same politics, but he said they just don't talk about it. They have a rent-controlled apartment and he named their Wi-Fi Fuckharper69, so his girlfriend started connecting to their neighbours' Wi-Fi instead.

"I can't be seen in that network," she said and I asked

Tyler if he was sure she was talking about the internet.

Tyler left Ottawa this morning in the dark to get me. When he picks me up, I'm wearing a pair of sweatpants that say QUEEN'S across the butt and Tyler tells me it looks ridiculous.

"Do you ever feel like you're just wasting Dad's money?" he asks once we are on the highway.

"I don't really think about it."

Our father has been married three times. The first time to his high school sweetheart, the second time to Tyler's mother and the third time to mine. My mother and father are still married and live on a cul-de-sac in Waterloo. When I was learning to drive, my father would sit in the passenger seat and I would drive around and around the cul-de-sac, not actually going anywhere. He would laugh and then get mad in a matter of seconds and then he would laugh again. This was the thing about my father, he never felt any particular way too intensely. Frank was this way too.

When I pretend to wake up, I put my hand over my mouth and yawn. The thing about a fake yawn, though, is it usually turns into a real one.

"Good nap?" Tyler asks and I know then that he doesn't take me seriously. But I think I've always known that.

"Mmmmm," I moan and think I sound exactly like a tired person.

When Tyler was twenty-five he moved in with us. He would sit in the basement and let his hair grow long. I was ten and thought Tyler hung the moon. He would let me do things that my parents wouldn't, like eat chocolate and play *Tony Hawk's Pro Skater*. He would pick me up from sleepovers in his silver Sunfire and we would listen to NOFX. His favourite song was "Bottles to the Ground" and I remember thinking,

Wow, this guy's cool. But I don't ever remember feeling like we were related, or like this person and I shared something as important as a father. I remember asking him what he wanted to do with his life and he didn't answer. But after that I always felt like he resented me or looked at me like I had more time and more ways to figure it out than he did.

I start feeling nauseous so I ask Tyler if we can stop at an ONroute. Frank and I haven't talked since Toronto. It's been two weeks and I didn't get my period at the end of the month and that's always when it comes. I think about taking a pregnancy test and then I think I'm fine just not knowing. Because once I know, I'll have to make a decision, and I'm just not good at that. I want to tell Tyler, but I know he'll say that making the decision is always easier. Getting rid of the choice is how people get happy.

I throw up at the ONroute and then I buy jelly beans and a green neck pillow with my father's credit card. I stand at the door waiting for Tyler to get a double-double. The ONroute is made of glass and has a Burger King and a Tim Hortons stemming from either side like arms. Tyler walks by me with his coffee and reaches out toward me as he's passing, like he's going to punch me in the stomach. At the last second he pulls away and keeps walking, but I still keel over, winded, like he's hurt me.

When we get back in the car I tell Tyler about how I recently started taking psychology classes and I don't understand it.

"That's weird. I always felt like you understood everything about everyone."

This is the nicest thing he's ever said to me. Tyler has never gone to university and after he moved out of our house on the court, he became a welder. "It just seemed easier to pick a thing and stick with it," he says. He just picked a girlfriend and a trade and a Wi-Fi password and he didn't think about it afterwards. I like this certainty about him.

"I think I'm pregnant."

Tyler lets go of the wheel and we swerve into the other lane. "I almost punched you in the stomach back there!"

"I know, I remember."

"I mean, of course I was kidding."

"Of course," I say. I open the car window and begin spitting the yellow jelly beans onto the highway like spitballs.

"Roxane, have you thought about this? Who is the father? That kid Frank?"

I look at one of the jelly beans as it leaves my mouth and I think that's probably the size of the fetus. "Tyler, just calm down. I'm a bit nauseous and I haven't gotten my period. That's it."

"You haven't taken a test?" he asks, and opens his window too, which begins to hurt my ears pretty quickly.

"No, I thought it was better to enjoy the weekend and think about it when I had to."

"Have you talked to Frank? What is he saying about all this?"

"Frank and I haven't spoken. We broke up at the AGO. Over an Alex Colville painting." Tyler whips his head around like he doesn't understand what I'm talking about. "You know, I started to think about family and God and everything and it really seems like Colville loved his wife so much and I just thought that I didn't love Frank like that. And then I started thinking about you and Dad and how close we all were, or if we were close at all. You know Dad made such huge decisions about marriage and kids when he was so young. It's kind of crazy when you think about it." I put the neck pillow on and it feels heavy. I wonder if Tyler and I can ever even feel fully related.

When I used to think about Tyler and our age difference I would think about it like two arms on a clock. He was always a quarter ahead of me. It was strange, now that I think about it, but it made me feel closer to him. Like I could see the two of us on the same face.

The only Thanksgiving we ever spent together was when I was eleven and Tyler was getting ready to move out of our house. I remember him grabbing my hand at the table and insisting we pray. The only ones who had faith were him and my mother.

"Maybe we should all say thank you for believing in each other," I'd said. I wanted it to be like church, when everyone shook hands with strangers. I knew this came after collection because I always remembered my father pulling a green twenty out of his pocket. The twenties in my father's wallet always looked like they had never been touched by anyone else before him. Tyler had taken this moment to go to the washroom and I wondered who it was he didn't believe in. That Thanksgiving I remember us all reaching in for the turkey, tearing its legs and wings off and stuffing them right in our mouths.

"I think I need to stop again. I feel sick."

He says there's an ONroute coming up and I drink a sip of his double double, which is cold and the sugar is at the bottom. I go straight to the bathroom, which I don't have trouble finding because it is in the exact same place as at the last ONroute where we stopped. I puke, and full jelly beans of all colours float around in the toilet, blending with each other. I think it's kind of beautiful before I flush. When I open the door Tyler is standing there with a pregnancy test.

"You have to take this." He holds it so close to my face it's almost touching my nose. "Trust me, you'll feel better when you know."

I move past him and say, "I want ice cream."

Between the Cheetos and the soft serve, Tyler starts to yell at me. He throws his arms up and the pregnancy test floats through the air like a baseball. He stares at me like he's waiting for me to react and suddenly he looks like a stranger.

"You don't even know me," I tell him as I wait for a woman in a hairnet to hand me my ice cream.

"I know that nothing has ever been difficult for you. Not really." I wonder if he is finally going to tell me he's angry that I got to grow up with our dad and he didn't. But he stops.

I wait for him at the door while he gets another double-double.

"This ONroute looks exactly the same as the last one," I tell Tyler when he is close enough to hear. I'm almost waiting for him to punch me in the stomach this time, so he can make the decision for me and I can stop sucking him into my world full of choices.

"Do you remember when you threw that pie in my face, at my ninth birthday?"

"Yeah, I remember."

"I felt really far away from you then," I say.

Tyler and I don't speak as we approach Toronto. I think about Frank's indifference toward me and how I inflated every good thing he ever said because I was surprised when he was nice. I think about Frank's parents, his father reading Homer and his mother thinking it was *The Simpsons*, Frank's father's hand in mine like he knew me. I wonder if Tyler thinks he was deprived of our father and if that's why he became religious.

We stop talking for a while and then right before Toronto, Tyler's car breaks down. I tell him I have Dad's CAA card and he rolls his eyes. I puke again on the side of the road and then call our father.

"We were moving and then all of a sudden we weren't going anywhere," I say over the phone. My father had taught me to drive in circles around the court, not going anywhere.

"Do you know where you are?"

I tell my father we are between two ONroutes that are organized the same way so I don't know where we are.

"Are you close to anything?" my father asks.

"I'm not sure."

A guy from CAA with long nose hair picks us up and we all squeeze into the front seat of a tow truck with me in the middle.

"You guys look a lot alike. You related?" the CAA man asks.

One of us says, "Yeah."

The other says, "Kinda."

STAYING ALIVE

When Olivia was six she fell in love with her baby-sitter, who was three times her age. His name was Daniel and he had blue eyes like her father. Daniel would always suggest they play games. His favourite was charades because he liked pretending he was someone else. Olivia told him she liked it too, although she wasn't sure. Sometimes they would play Monopoly and Daniel would always buy the cheapest properties. He said he couldn't be trusted with Park Place. When they played Connect Four, Daniel would always let Olivia win.

"Nothing ever connects, Olivia, remember that," he would say.

There was something sad about Daniel that made Olivia want to hold him, like he was the child. She wished she was older so that would be okay. Daniel would tell Olivia that she had a baby face. She never knew what this meant and it wasn't how she saw herself. Olivia was confident in a way that was not just projected. Her mother's friends would come over and say, "You know, confidence is the best thing you can give a child." Her mother would agree and pick up a hand weight.

Daniel had just started going to King's College and he would walk to Olivia's family's house on Connaught Avenue after he finished Intro to Philosophy. He had grown up in St. John's and he thought Halifax was huge. He would tell Olivia about Homer and Heidegger and Dante and Derrida and Olivia would rush to her room and sound out the names, writing them in her journal like secrets that she never wanted to forget. She felt challenged by Daniel, which was important since she so rarely felt challenged by the people around her. They treated her like a baby and Daniel treated her like something more than that.

Olivia was eight when Daniel took her to see *An Inconvenient Truth*. After it was over, he smoked a cigarette outside the Oxford Theatre and then he smoked another one. His hands were shaking and it scared her. It snowed then and he bent down at a ninety-degree angle with his cigarette still hanging from his mouth. He was blowing smoke into the air and Olivia looked up to see where it was all going. He pulled her scarf tighter around her neck and said, "We'll all be dead soon. This planet just can't sustain us all."

Olivia's father was a doctor and her mother was a trainer. They both had next to no body fat and they had recently stopped eating fish and meat and dairy. Her mother ate spinach with no dressing and always wore leggings, like she was ready to run. Her parents would go to the gym together in the mornings and sometimes at night.

"Your father and I are trying to see who can lose thirty pounds the fastest," her mother said one day after opening a tin of tuna for Olivia.

"That seems like a lot of weight."

"We're just trying to live longer, sweetie!"

Her mother walked away from her and Olivia could see the step counter on her wrist light up like she had reached her goal.

"Mom, do you ever get sick of all this health stuff?" Olivia yelled.

She could hear her mother climbing the stairs. "Well, if I stopped, that would be like putting a gun in my mouth and pulling the trigger, Livy!"

Olivia finished the tuna and cleaned out the tin like her mother had showed her.

When Daniel came over he would bring Sour Patch Kids and root beer and they would ride the city bus downtown. On Spring Garden, Daniel would hold Olivia's hand until they got to the Public Gardens and then Olivia would run ahead. He would chase her down the gravel path until Olivia bent over, her little hands on her knees and say, "I'm tired."

"Your parents would be proud of you. You're getting your cardio in!"

Olivia would always laugh when he was trying to be funny, because she loved him. Daniel would sometimes run into people he knew and his friends would pat her on the head and call her kid. Sometimes Daniel would call her kid too, which Olivia hated.

Olivia would always ask Daniel to talk to her about school. So he would talk to her about Freud's superego and not being able to have what you desire. He would talk about Nietzsche and the forbidden. He would talk about how we all had to unlearn and forget so we could figure out how to grow into new people that can get what they want out of life.

When she was ten, Olivia's parents got a golden retriever and named it Kale. They said the dog was going to make them happy and fill them up. Olivia wondered what prompted getting the dog because her parents were not dog people. But one night in October she overheard them in the living room talking about having another child, and everything started to make sense.

"Do you think we should see a fertility specialist?" her mother asked, and it sounded like she was eating, which added to the fraudulence of the memory. Her father said that the problem probably had to do with their fitness. And Olivia thought about her mother's self-regulation and how she just wanted to take care of something else other than herself.

Olivia told Daniel to meet her at Sears in the mall and told him to bring snacks. Daniel showed up with Sour Patch Kids. He said that he had remembered they were her favourite. Olivia had just graduated high school and her friend group had started hanging out at the mall a lot. When Daniel arrived, Olivia was in the furniture section, lying in a kids' double bed with pink and purple striped sheets. She patted the spot beside her and rolled down the covers. Daniel turned his head sideways. Olivia thought he looked handsome.

"I don't think we should be doing this."

"Doing what? C'mon, it's fun to pretend you're a kid."

"That's funny. I remember you hating it," he said.

Daniel got under the covers like he would when he tucked Olivia in years ago, when her mother paid him eight dollars an hour. When he got under the sheets Olivia turned sideways and hugged her knees.

"How are you?" she asked. She hadn't seen him in years,

before last week, when she ran into him at the new public library downtown. He was sitting in a red chair against a white wall, reading *War and Peace*. She remembered when he stopped babysitting her like it was yesterday. Her mother had caught him smoking on the back patio one night when she got home from the gym and raised her voice and told him he was killing himself.

Daniel told Olivia that he stopped going to school and that he moved back to Newfoundland. He said that it was easier there to just pretend you existed separately from all the terrifying stuff.

"Remember when you took me to see *An Inconvenient Truth*?"

"Yeah." He opened the Sour Patch Kids and they flew all over the bed. "The truth really scared me back then."

"I know. I remember."

Olivia picked up a yellow Sour Patch Kid and sucked on it until it was slimy. "You used to hate the yellow ones," she reminded him.

Daniel smiled and for the first time in her life she realized his age. He had little lines around his eyes that she thought were inevitable with how much he worried. They looked like little maps, which she thought was ironic since she'd never met anyone so lost.

He stood up and ran his hands through his thick brown hair. "I'm gonna go out and smoke," he said.

Olivia fixed the bed and ate the remaining Sour Patch Kids that were trickled on the mattress. She followed Daniel outside and said, "Can I bum one off of you?"

He laughed and threw his head back so she could see his soft chin.

"You're a kid."

"I'm eighteen."

He handed her a smoke between two fingers and said, "That is terrifying."

When Olivia got home her mother was watching *The Good Wife*, which she had recently started marathoning on Netflix. She always marvelled at how the couple in the show were able to stay together when he couldn't give her what she wanted.

"Where's Kale?" Olivia asked.

Her mother looked unwell. Her face had sunken in over time and she looked hungry. She had gotten lip fillers and it looked like someone had punched her in the face.

"Where's Dad?"

"He's upstairs."

Her dad came down the stairs seconds later with Kale chasing his heels. "Honey!" Her father put his hands over her ears and kissed her on the forehead. "I'm going to take the dog for a walk to the grocery store. Want to join me?"

Olivia's father was handsome in a way that was obvious. Most of the time he looked like he had just gotten off a sailboat. His age hadn't caught up with him in the same way it had caught up to her mother, which seemed unfair.

It had started raining and all the colours of the stores were reflected on the wet road like a painting. Her father walked slightly in front of her and asked her about school and dance and her friend Natasha. Olivia always had these conversations with her father. It was like a checklist that they ran through to make sure things were in order. People told Olivia she looked like her father. But Olivia thought it was just because they were similar. Both of them made things look effortless, which her mother had a harder time doing. When Olivia was younger she would move all her food to different corners of her plate and eat the food separately. This was when her parents still ate potatoes. Her mother would tell her she should eat it all at once because there was more flavour and her father told her to figure it out herself. She always felt more freedom with her dad. Olivia was wearing a shiny yellow raincoat and suddenly she felt like a child. They left Kale outside and Olivia and her father entered the Atlantic Superstore.

Olivia and Natasha had come here a few weeks before to get gin. They waited outside the Superstore for a person who looked nice enough to buy them alcohol. It was a flawed system but Natasha swore it would work. The man they asked said he was a police officer and they should be getting home. The way he looked at them made Olivia feel younger than she ever had before.

Her father rushed to the produce aisle and Olivia told him to wait up. Their shoes squeaked on the tiled floor as Olivia watched him bag everything separately. There was an inflatable palm tree hanging above the pineapples. The forecast was calling for snow.

They waited to pay behind a bunch of college students who looked the same. Daniel never looked like these kids. She thought about his soft chin and him handing her a cigarette. "I saw Daniel today," Olivia told her father.

"No way! How's he doing?"

"He's good. He's thirty."

"Ah, yes, we're all getting up there."

"Up where?" Olivia said and her father laughed.

Her father asked her if she wanted to stop at McDonald's on the way back home.

"Are you serious?"

Her father stayed outside with Kale and insisted that he shouldn't eat when Olivia asked him if he wanted anything. Olivia got chicken nuggets to go, with fries and three packs of sweet and sour. She had always ordered the same thing as a kid when Daniel would take her to get fast food.

"Ready to go?" she asked her father as she walked out into the rain.

When they were standing under the golden arches—her father bathed in a yellow light—he turned to Olivia and said, "I have prostate cancer."

Olivia choked on a long and flimsy fry she had snuck from the bag and barely chewed. It flew out of her mouth and onto the sidewalk by her father's shoe. It looked the same as before she had eaten it.

"I'm sorry, honey."

"Is it serious?"

She was holding a chicken nugget and it suddenly felt like a hand weight. Everything immediately felt heavier. Even the rain started to feel like it was stabbing her head as it fell. Her father moved them to the bench outside the McDonald's and Olivia stuffed a chicken nugget in her mouth. She chewed on it for what seemed like minutes.

"They're going to do surgery and after that I should be able to return to life as normal."

"Well, that's good, right?"

"It is. But there's some risk involved." Her dad paused and grabbed one of the fries from her bag. She hadn't ever seen her father eat fried food and she wondered if his time for discipline was over now that he was sick.

"I might lose urinary control." He paused. "And I could experience erectile disfunction."

Olivia didn't know what to say. She hadn't been thinking of her parents as human beings who could get sick and scared. She never thought about them having sex and she definitely never thought about them dying. "What's Mom saying? Does she want you to get the surgery?"

"Your mother is terrified of death, sweetie." He ate another fry. "Which I'm sure you probably know."

"I guess," Olivia said. She did know that, but she never thought about her mother's craziness as being a reaction against losing something.

"I don't know. It's like all the things that make me a man are being threatened right now," he said.

Olivia put her head on her dad's shoulder and said, "We're all losing youth all the time."

"You're not losing me."

"No. Youth, not you."

The next day Olivia called Daniel and asked what he was doing. She told him she would pick him up and they could cross the bridge to the other side. He asked her to clarify and she said, "Dartmouth."

She picked him up from his apartment in the South End and when he got in the car he said, "I can't believe you can drive."

"Why?"

"Well, you're just so young. You're just a kid."

Olivia drove them to the Macdonald Bridge in her mother's Lexus and asked Daniel if he had change. He pulled a toonie from the back pocket of his Levi's and halfway over the bridge Olivia said, "I think my dad is going to die." She told him about the prostate cancer and her father eating fries. Daniel said he was surprised by both. Olivia drove down the highway until the airport and said, "Let's just stop here."

They got double-doubles from Tim Hortons and sat by the cargo garage, parallel to the runway. Daniel was talking about dropping out of school and feeling like it was a waste of time. He wanted to do things that felt more immediate and he missed St. John's. He said he just hadn't been ready to leave home when he was seventeen because there was still so much for him to learn that wasn't Derrida. And he never got a chance to figure out what it was he really wanted to do because he was too busy reading and taking care of her.

"I'm sorry," Olivia said.

"Don't be," he whispered, and took a sip of his coffee. "You're what kept me here so long. I really loved taking care of you. And I really needed the money."

"I loved it too."

A plane flew above the car and Olivia said, "Tell me about Newfoundland."

Daniel said it was different from anywhere else. The people were nicer and more understanding. He talked about the houses all connected like a bunch of handshakes and said, "I think you'd like it."

"Yeah?"

"No one there ever makes you feel bad for feeling confused. It's like everywhere else I've lived there's been this competition to see who can graduate first and who can get published before they're twenty. People notice who has the nicest jean jacket and people wonder who will live the longest.

But at home that stuff matters less. Or it feels like it matters less."

"None of that has ever really mattered to me," Olivia said.

"I know. It's what makes you special. It's like you exist outside of the rules or the boundaries or something. You've always been like that." He paused and fiddled with his lighter. The flame kept coming and going. "It's like you're free of something big," Daniel said and he lit a cigarette in her mom's car. He gave her one too and the car became smoky enough that she could barely see him. She reached her hand out to touch his chest and it felt fine as long as she couldn't see him.

Friday night, while she was drunk, Olivia called Daniel from campus. She walked out into the middle of the King's quad and sat down cross-legged like a kid. She looked at the buildings around her and thought about tradition and how she'd mostly come to this school because of Daniel. She still had the notebooks that she'd filled with ideas about philosophy and Daniel. She wanted to feel the same way he did, burdened and emotional and attached to things. She wanted to feel bothered by the world.

"Hey? Olivia? Are you okay?"

"I'm at this party at King's," she said. "It's themed Dante's Inferno and all the different floors of the residence represent the different levels of hell."

Daniel laughed through the phone and said, "I can't believe they're still doing that."

"Can you come pick me up?"

"Sure. I'll be there in ten."

"Thank you," she said. "This is seriously hell."

Daniel picked Olivia up in the Toyota Corolla he shared

with his best friend Matt and took her back to his apartment and told her to be quiet because his roommates were sleeping. His bedroom was at the end of the hallway and when they walked in there was a yoga mat on the floor and an exercise ball that he used as a desk chair. Olivia lay on the yoga mat and Daniel sat on his bed.

"Sorry, I was working out before I came to pick you up."

Olivia laughed and said, "Do you think this shit really works?"

"I don't know. It makes me feel better, I think."

"Why, though?"

"I just don't want to go soft."

"I think I'm going to puke," she said, running to the bathroom.

Daniel followed her and pulled her hair back when she puked, like he did when she was a kid. Olivia's puke was red and it almost looked like blood.

"Jesus," Daniel said.

"Don't worry, it was just the martinis. They were themed."

Daniel sat down beside her and leaned against the bathtub. Olivia put her feet on his lap and she knew that it made him uncomfortable. "Thank you for taking care of me," she said.

"I used to do it all the time." He took her sock off and rubbed her foot. She wondered if he had finally stopped thinking of her as a kid. The bathroom was silent except for the faucet that was still dripping slightly so the pipes didn't freeze.

"Why did you come back here?" Olivia asked.

"I guess I always felt best when I was taking care of you."

"But you were always miserable. And scared of everything."

"No I wasn't," Daniel said. He smiled.

Olivia moved so she was sitting beside Daniel with their backs against the bathtub. She leaned over and kissed him on the mouth. He tasted like cigarette smoke and also sweat and she thought that made sense. He was always killing himself and trying to save himself at the same time. When she pulled away she noticed that his eyebrows were going grey.

"Olivia," he whispered. "I don't want to be with you."

"What?"

He tucked a piece of hair behind her ear like he didn't want anything to be out of place. "I'm jealous of you—there's a difference."

Olivia didn't think there was a difference. Her parents and Daniel were existing in a world where everything was fleeting and whoever could hold onto life the longest was the one who would win. But Olivia was looking to hold onto something different, something meaningful. She really believed that people could love the wrong thing and still be okay. And maybe Daniel didn't believe that, but she wanted him to. She thought about the board games they used to play and how Daniel loved charades the best and how he loved to pretend. She remembered how he called her kid and still pretended that she was one. Olivia puked once more before she got up and left.

"Hey, I was just playing," Daniel said, reaching for her hand.

"I don't want to play. I'm too old." She descended three floors. Her legs felt shaky like nothing she had depended on would hold her up anymore.

When Olivia got home her parents were having takeout. Her father was eating McDonald's nuggets out of the bag and it made Olivia cry silent tears that fell off her cheeks and onto the Persian rug her mother had brought back from Vancouver years ago.

"Sweetie?"

Olivia wiped her eyes and sat between her parents. She told them she wished they were both bigger and softer so she could hold onto them better.

UNDECLARED

Joy and her mother drove toward the border, weaving in and out of the fast lane, sunshine illuminating their laps hardly at all and then all at once. Joy had just finished a bag of Party Mix right down to the bottom and her fingers were a dusty orange—almost yellow—like she was a lifelong smoker. She tried wiping them on the front seat of her mother's Windstar without her noticing.

When they approached the border, the sun disappeared, and Joy's bones felt colder. She pulled their passports out of her mother's purse on the floor in the front seat and left an orange fingerprint right on her mother's nose on the picture page.

That fall, Joy had started seeing a married man who taught her Contemporary American Fiction Class at Queen's. His name was Gary and he was balding, right at the top of his head in a perfect circle. Gary was smart and he taught Joy about the recklessness of living under late capitalism. Sometimes he would come to her apartment and read *American Psycho* and tuck her into bed like she was a child. He would tell her he was leaving his wife and that he liked Joy's collarbone, the weightlessness of her past.

Joy's mother had taken her to Buffalo for the day, a trip they'd been taking once a year since Joy was a kid. When she turned thirteen, her mother started encouraging Joy to wear clothes she hated or knew she would soon throw out for the trip down, and because each person could only declare two hundred dollars a day, Joy and her mother would go to the bathroom at the Cheesecake Factory in Buffalo and throw their old clothes in the garbage and rip the tags off the new ones, leaving them undeclared.

Joy had been looking for a way to tell her mother about Gary all day. She also wanted to tell her that she got so drunk the first week of frosh that she stopped seeing straight. She wanted to tell her that she'd gotten an IUD at Planned Parenthood and she had been bleeding for months. She wanted her mother to pat her head, right on the top, and tell her this was all normal and okay.

Their customs officer, Anita, was an older woman with two pimples, one right under her nose and another on her chin. After some questioning, she got Joy's mother to pull the Windstar to a small parking lot on the Canadian side of the border and she searched their car. Anita started losing breath as she leaned into the trunk, swiping her arms under the seat for evidence of things left undeclared. Joy wondered why Anita had picked them to screen and thought it might have something to do with women not trusting each other.

While Anita was rummaging through the trunk, Joy's mother looked at her and smiled like everything they were in on, they were in on together. Anita shut the trunk with surprising strength and looked at Joy critically. She may have just been judging her outfit; the mix of colours and patterns making no sense.

"Are you sure your daughter's not hiding anything, ma'am?"

Joy couldn't look at her mother then. She just gazed at her feet, thinking about how her mother was perfect and beautiful and honest.

"Of course not, Anita, we tell each other everything," her mother said.

IT'S GETTING DARK OUT

This was the week that Donald Trump won the presidency. It was the same week that Lucy broke up with Mitch.

He asked her why and she said, "I just can't stay optimistic anymore."

When Lucy went home that night, her father was wearing a red ball cap. On the front in white Times New Roman font it said MAKE AMERICA GREAT AGAIN. Her father was watching CNN with his feet up and started talking loudly to no one about the liberal news media. One hand held the remote and the other controlled his chair.

"Hi, Dad."

"Hey, honey. You hungry? Want a drink? I'm feeling celebratory."

"I'm fine, thank you."

Lucy went to her room and cried. When she got up, there was a wet face mark on the pillow and she turned it over, remembering how easy it used to be to solve a problem. When you can't sleep, turn the pillow over.

Lucy called Mitch. "I can't stop crying."

"Maybe it's good."

"What do you mean? How could it be good?"

"Maybe everyone will like stop pretending now."

Lucy said she didn't want that. She thought pretending was how people kept going. She told herself pretending was different from lying but sometimes she didn't know.

"Don't you think there's something admirable about your dad not pretending? He likes Donald Trump, and it would be a lot easier for you if he didn't. But he's not pretending he doesn't like him. He wants you to know. He's wearing the hat, for God's sake."

"But isn't anyone who likes Donald Trump pretending because the whole platform of his appeal is kinda fake? He doesn't know anything."

"But people like that. Because he's not lying to himself. Maybe anyone who knows anything is just lying to themselves and to everyone else."

"I don't think that makes sense," Lucy said.

"I know you don't."

The next day Lucy and Mitch went to the Dollarama. The sky was pink overhead. They sat in the parking lot and she told Mitch she thought that the dollar store was breaking its promise because everything inside wasn't just a dollar.

"Everyone breaks their promises," he said.

Lucy grabbed his hand and they stared at the moms entering Dollarama in puffy black coats to their ankles.

"I'm sorry I broke up with you," Lucy whispered.

Mitch didn't respond. He turned the radio on to NPR, where the announcer had started talking about Hillary Clinton's popular vote lead.

Mitch started nodding his head and talking about the

electoral college. "It's insane. The winner is the one who loses."

Suddenly there was a crash. A black SUV ran into Mitch's tail light and Mitch swore really loudly. He stepped out and talked to the man in the SUV. They were just two dark shadows against the pink sky and for a second Lucy thought it was beautiful. When she got out of the car, she could see it was getting dark out.

"He asked me about the election," Mitch said, bringing a strawberry vape to his mouth with shaky hands.

"Who did?"

"The man who ran into my tail light!"

"What did he say about it?"

"He said he doesn't know how to exist now."

She looked to her left and she could see the CN Tower. There were people balancing near the top, their bodies hanging over the city, their arms up. This was the city's newest adventure: the EdgeWalk.

Mitch looked at Lucy looking at the CN Tower.

"Why do people do this?" Lucy asked.

"They want to feel the thrill, I guess. Or the freedom, or something," Mitch said.

Lucy told him she always felt like she was walking on the edge of something and she would never dream of doing the EdgeWalk. She didn't understand why people wanted to feel out of control. She didn't understand why people wanted revolution. She didn't want things to feel threatened.

It was Saturday night and they were in Mitch's bed at his new apartment in the junction. They hadn't had sex since before the election and that's how Lucy was thinking about it: Before and After. She handed Mitch a condom and he said, "We haven't used a condom in months."

"I'm not taking any chances," Lucy said.

"But you have an IUD."

"I got it removed yesterday."

"Why?"

"Because everything felt like it was unravelling and I was just thinking about how I have this like metal thing in my vagina and how I haven't had a period in years and I guess I just wanted to bleed, or something."

"But I don't want to use a condom."

Lucy looked at Mitch and for a second she almost felt bad for him. She felt bad that he didn't bleed. That he never thought about going on a diet. She felt bad that he never cried and he didn't think about it. It was all so easy.

Lucy rolled off him and said, "I don't feel like having sex right now." She didn't want anyone inside her when she was this uncertain.

Mitch didn't respond, just sat up in bed, against a white wall with nothing on it, and called his insurance company. They explained that his insurance would go up and Mitch kept repeating that he hadn't done anything. The insurance company said that because he was a man, his insurance was already higher than if he was a woman. Lucy could hear them explaining this through the phone and she saw Mitch roll his eyes like he didn't understand why he had it so hard.

Lucy put her feet on the ground, a chill running through her because Mitch refused to pay the heat bill. She put her pants on and then realized she hadn't eaten in days, since before the election, but she didn't feel hungry.

Lucy called an Uber and when she got in her Uber driver

handed her a Ziploc bag of white powder and she said, "I just wanted you to take me home."

The Uber driver explained that he was a drug dealer and not an Uber driver so Lucy switched cars.

Mitch texted her, "I could have driven you home."

Lucy sent him a heart emoji and said, "Your tail light is smashed." "Tail light" autocorrected to "twilight" and Mitch sent her back a question mark to which Lucy didn't respond.

Lucy's best friend, Emily, came over the next morning and said she was going to try acting. Emily went to the University of Toronto for sociology and lived with five strangers in the West End. Emily had just painted her room all white and hung a picture of Lucy in the middle of the wall. Emily was strict and sad and God, she was pretty.

"Do you really want to do this?" Lucy said.

Emily flopped on Lucy's bed like she was doing a trust fall. She propped her head on her hand and stared at Lucy.

"I think this is a new time for entertainment."

"I don't know what you mean."

"America just elected an entertainer! They want to be entertained! And why can't I entertain them? I feel like everyone is going to start acting now, right?"

Lucy heard CNN downstairs. She thought about how Mitch said people were tired of pretending and that's why Donald Trump was president. As she crawled into bed with Emily and pulled the comforter over them, she said, "Emily, you want to be a professional pretender?"

"What about school?"

"Ugh. I'm just tired of trying to understand people."

Emily was working on a project where she studied people

at airport checkpoints. She went to Pearson every day and sat outside security by the Starbucks and wrote about how people acted at these places of transition. Sometimes Lucy would go along too for a laugh. They would drink half-sweet caramel macchiatos and sit cross-legged on the tile floor until they were told to leave. Emily would tell the security people she was writing a thesis, which sometimes worked. Lucy thought this was because Emily was beautiful and most people had a hard time saying no to beautiful people.

"We should go to the airport," Lucy said as she started playing with a loose thread on the duvet her mother left behind. "It might make me feel better to analyze something outside of myself."

"Lucy, are you listening to me? I said I don't want to do that anymore. I want to act."

Emily was being irrational. Lucy wondered if it was the first time she had lost her head.

"I broke up with Mitch."

"What? Why?"

"I was feeling sad about the world."

Emily laid her head down on the pillow and for a second Lucy thought she looked like an angel. "Fine. Let's go to the airport."

Lucy asked Emily if she could drive. They took the Gardiner but there was construction all the way to Brown's Line. She felt good speeding down the road. She'd gotten her licence after her father had moved to an apartment in the Beaches. This was after her mother admitted she was done pretending. Lucy had wanted to tell her that pretending was how people kept going but she knew that wouldn't have made her stay.

"They must be widening the highway," Emily said.

"They've been widening the highway for six years. They want to build express lanes."

Emily laughed and slurped a grape slushy they'd stopped for back on Queen out of a huge 7-Eleven cup. Emily always got grape and it made her teeth and her tongue purple.

The two lawn chairs Emily always brought on these trips sat between them like a divider. The lawn chairs were green like the grass that Lucy's parents used to sit on as the girls played T-ball. Their helmets were always too big and would fall over their eyes like a blindfold. Lucy's father would laugh and he would pick Lucy up and throw her over his shoulder until she was dizzy. She wondered when her father stopped being happy. Or maybe he was still happy but just in a different way. She wondered if supporting a politician she believed was bad made her father bad and if he'd become different after her mother left.

"Do you think you know your parents?" Lucy asked.

"Yeah. I mean, I've been studying them for years," Emily said, slurping the last sip of her slushy.

Lucy suddenly wondered if Emily's inclination to study people for school was what would make her a good actor.

"I remember always thinking they were going to get divorced. When I was growing up. I remember they would fight and they would do things like turn on the blender so I wouldn't hear. But I think they were always still happy even when they weren't happy with each other."

"That's amazing," Lucy said.

Emily nodded her head and turned on the radio. The station was talking about Hillary's campaign mistakes in Wisconsin so she turned it off again.

"I never remember my parents fighting," Lucy said. "Or maybe I just wasn't listening."

"I think you avoid looking at certain things if those things aren't what you want to see."

Lucy looked at Emily and bit the inside of her cheeks until her face looked hollow.

"I think you're right."

Lucy set up the two green lawn chairs outside security by the elevator. She sat down and crossed her legs and she felt better.

"I like doing this. It's comforting," Lucy said.

"I know. But why?"

"I don't know, I guess it's nice to see people like this."

"Like what?"

"Like scared. People have to like prove their identities and then show all their things to someone else and convince them they're trustworthy."

"Yeah." Emily wrapped her legs like a pretzel underneath her and pulled out a notebook, purple like her mouth. "You're seeing someone go somewhere and leave somewhere at the same time."

Lucy smiled and thought that was exactly right.

The woman working security came up to them and encouraged them to leave. Emily begged her to pretend they weren't there to which she replied with indifference.

Everyone acted a certain way when they got to security. It was comforting to watch because there were almost never surprises. Lucy wondered how many places were like that. She wanted to stay there forever, watching people whose behaviour she could predict. Beside her, Emily was taking bullet point notes in cursive writing and she wondered if

Emily was the last person on earth who wrote in cursive. In a place where everyone was proving their identity, Lucy grabbed Emily's hand. Their hands linked above the arm of the lawn chair, where there was a cup holder.

"I think you should act," Lucy said.

Lucy booked an appointment at Planned Parenthood the following week for a new IUD. It was expensive but when she told Mitch he said he would pay half.

He drove to her father's house in his car with the smashed tail light and her dad said, "Mitch, you should follow the law."

Mitch nodded and said, "I know, sir."

It was always strange to watch them interact. They were a lot alike and Lucy wondered if that's why she resisted needing Mitch.

"How 'bout that election, hey, son," her father said, offering Mitch a Coors Light from the fridge like he would a handshake.

"It's pretty unbelievable." Mitch made a comment about how they were lucky to live in Canada and how this stuff shouldn't really affect people as much as they were letting it.

Lucy left the room so they wouldn't know she was crying and began cutting an onion with the Jamie Oliver knife her father won with stamps. This made her cry more.

"Do you even like Donald Trump, Dad?" Lucy yelled from the kitchen.

"Well, obviously I don't think he's a great man but that doesn't have anything to do with his platform. He's completely unqualified, but look how he won. He just told the truth."

Lucy cut her thumb with the knife and swore.

Her father said, "What, honey? You don't agree?"

"No, I just cut myself." Blood was dripping onto the salmon-coloured linoleum. Mitch jumped up and wrapped Lucy's hand with his own and said, "You have to apply pressure or it won't stop."

"What won't?" Lucy asked.

Mitch stared at her and squinted like he didn't understand her anymore. "The bleeding."

Emily called that night and asked if she could stay over at Lucy's. "My roommate is having a house show and he asked if I could remove my boots before entering."

Lucy laughed and agreed so Emily said, "I'll take the subway."

Lucy picked Emily up from Main Station—like always—and Emily said, "Jesus, what happened to your hand?"

"Oh, I cut it with my dad's Jamie Oliver knife."

"Did you go to the hospital?"

"No. Mitch just wrapped it in a napkin and held my hand for a few hours."

"That sounds . . . nice."

Lucy thought about grabbing Emily's hand in the airport and how it had made her feel warm inside. They drove the rest of the way in silence before Emily said, "Does Mitch make you happy?"

Lucy didn't know how to respond so instead she went on a tangent about how the promise of happiness was fake and then put the car in park.

Lucy's room was dark and she felt Emily turn over toward the wall. "I miss when we were kids," Lucy said. The past felt so much easier than any future she could imagine.

"I know, and your mom would wake us up and make us smoothies with yogurt."

"I wonder what she's doing now."

"I don't know. Hopefully she's happy." The room went quiet except for the heater that rattled in the corner.

"I hope she's not happy," Lucy said, and hearing the words out loud made her sad.

"Think about how much better it would have been if she had just told you the truth."

Lucy reached backwards and turned on the lamp beside the bed. She kissed Emily on her perfect purple mouth and she turned the light off.

The next day when Mitch took her out to the Beacher for breakfast, Lucy ate a sausage and told him they should stop seeing each other.

"What?"

"I don't think we should be together."

"But what about last night?"

"You held my hand to stop my thumb from bleeding."

"Yeah, but it stopped, right?"

Mitch looked young to her now, like a boy or like a baby. His hair was pushed to the side like he had forced it that way and his eyes were red. Lucy thought he was going to cry and she was surprised by that.

"Everything is just going to shit," he said.

"You're right," Lucy agreed.

She stuck a hash brown in her mouth and thought about getting really fat. Her thumb hurt and so did her uterus. She wondered if she was going crazy and why she had kissed

Emily. Was she pretending this whole time that her sexuality was one thing and moved in one way? Was she pretending that history or family had a way of moving forward in a line that made sense? Because she now mostly understood that these things didn't ever make sense, because not everyone was telling the truth.

Emily didn't speak to Lucy for a week and when Lucy asked her to go for sushi Emily told her she had an audition.

Her father passed her room and asked her where Emily was.

"She's acting."

For her birthday, after she blew out the candles, her father gave her a card. He had showered and his hair was combed back with what Lucy thought was gel. He was wearing a brown-and-red checkered shirt and she asked him if he'd shaved.

"Yeah! I guess I did."

Lucy hugged him and said, "You smell like you did when I was young." Lucy loved the smell of her father's aftershave but it used to make her mom sick to her stomach.

Her father's card had big bubbly cursive writing on the front that made her think about Emily. Inside was a gift certificate to the EdgeWalk.

"I thought we could do it together. I hear it's amazing. You can see the whole city!"

Lucy looked at her father and wondered if he knew her at all or if he just pretended and treated her like a father is supposed to treat a daughter. She had been alive a quarter of a century and he still hadn't figured her out.

That weekend Lucy hung above the city from a harness. She wore a helmet and thought, *God, I hate this*. Her father was beside her and he reached out and grabbed her hand. It made her thumb hurt where it was still healing but she smiled at him anyway.

"Happy birthday!" he yelled. "Look down, honey! You can see everything! Isn't this fun?"

"Yeah, Dad. It is."

NO MAN'S LAND

I n her senior year, Beverly discovered the fall of man. Her school was putting on a production of *Paradise Lost*, but Adam and Eve would both be played by women. And Satan too. This was an executive decision made by Beverly's drama teacher, who had recently made it a habit of using language like *slay, queen* and *lady boss*. She insisted everyone call her Rebecca. Rebecca said she suffered some pushback from the school administrators, who didn't think she should be erasing men from history. When Rebecca told this part of the story she started laughing until she was so red in the face Beverly thought she might puke.

One night in May, Beverly chipped her tooth on a bottle of Black Horse. Steve's father operated the Aquarena and told Steve that Wednesday they would be emptying the pool and replacing all the water with clean stuff. Steve told Beverly and Ginny and Ryan that he would pick them up at ten and he would get a case of beer with his fake. The girls rode in the back and Beverly could see that Ginny had put on eyeliner that twirled at the end of her eye like a wave. Ryan was vaping without the window cracked and the smoke was filling the car with the smell of watermelon.

"Did your parents name you after Virginia Woolf?" Beverly asked and couldn't believe she didn't know.

"Yeah, I guess," Ginny said, like she didn't care. "I've only ever read *The Waves* though."

"Did you know that Virginia Woolf drowned herself?"

"Shit," Ginny said and put her head out the window like a dog.

"She did a lot for women though!"

When they got to the pool it was completely empty. Steve jumped in and leaned against the wall.

"This is so weird, dude. Remember when we used to come here for lessons?"

Beverly nodded and said she remembered. Steve was her oldest friend. Their families were close and she and Steve were baptized on the same day. Beverly's mother had recently shown her a photo of the two of them held beside each other, their hair wet from water, crying like babies.

"We're always doing water activities together," Beverly said.

"I wouldn't consider baptism an activity." Steve took a huge slug of his beer and it reminded her of the way her dad drank on the weekends. He handed her a Black Horse and Beverly took off the cap and put it in her pocket. She tucked her hair behind her ear and winced. Yesterday, she and Ginny had gone to Churchill Square and bought vanilla dip doughnuts and then they got their ears pierced at Studio Maxx. Beverly had held Ginny's hand tight and Ginny said, "We could have just used a needle and an apple."

"Dude, we should bring our skateboards here though,"

Ryan shouted at Steve.

Steve gave Ryan a thumbs-up and Beverly sat down beside him. Ginny and Ryan had just started dating and they were making out in the shallow end. Ginny looked up. Her eyeliner was smudged.

"It looks like she has a black eye," Steve said as he cracked open another beer and threw the cap toward the shallow end.

"Are you sure this is okay? That we're here? Your dad won't be mad?"

"Just stop worrying for one second. We're fine." He grabbed her hand and turned it around in his like it was something he'd never seen before.

"I feel like this is what Rebecca is trying to do to our minds. Empty them out and replace all the problematic stuff with clean stuff." Beverly gestured at the empty pool so he would know what she was talking about.

Steve laughed. "You're insane," he said.

Beverly finished her first beer and felt her face turn red.

"Hey, you got your ear pierced." He moved her hair aside, making her feel hot all over.

It had only been the last little while that Steve had been making her feel this way, like he wanted something from her but he was too scared to ask. They were graduating in the spring and Beverly had just accepted her offer to go to Toronto Metropolitan University. Her parents had thrown her a party when she got accepted and they got a cake. Steve's family had come over early and Steve had been wearing a tie with polka dots. As she bent over and blew the candles out, her hair caught on fire. Steve put the flame out with a washcloth and said, "I'm proud of you, Bev."

"Are you going to try out for the play?" Steve asked.

"I guess. Rebecca told me she's feeling really bummed out and she only wants to be around women. She wants us to feel like we exist for each other and not for men and how she thinks it's bullshit that Eve came from Adam's rib, you know." Beverly took a sip of Steve's beer. "I don't know, the whole thing seems a bit crazy to me."

Steve agreed and said something about how pushing her feminism on her students was kinda weird. Ginny and Ryan held hands as they walked back toward the deep end and they all sat in a circle as they finished the beer. Beverly was feeling drunk after her third Black Horse and started to do summersaults and cartwheels down one lane of the pool until she reached the other end. On her final summersault she got dizzy and hit her mouth against an almost empty beer bottle. Her front tooth chipped halfway down and half the tooth now sat on the bottom of the pool against the shiny blue tile. Everyone paused waiting for her reaction. Beverly covered her mouth with her hand and started laughing. Steve started laughing too and he picked up the piece of tooth and put it in his pocket.

"What am I going to tell my parents?!" Beverly was kneeling on the pool floor now and she smiled. "Oh my God, can you see my tongue?"

Steve said, "I feel like I can see all the way back to your brain." He paused. "I like it."

Beverly's parents noticed her pierced ear before they noticed her tooth. When they finally saw the gap in her mouth, her father told her it was fine and that she just needed a cap.

"What's that?" Beverly asked.

"It's like a cover-up. So you don't see what's underneath."

"What are people going to think?" Beverly asked. Her voice was shaking and she was getting overwhelmed.

"Honey, who cares? It will look the same as before."

Beverly had never cared about her appearance when she was younger. She wanted to care about things that were bigger than that, like her mind. But lately she had been feeling small and vain and interested in looking good. She wanted to think it had nothing to do with Steve but she wasn't sure.

Beverly's father had just bought a vape in his quest to stop smoking and he liked the blueberry flavour the best. So he was vaping in the house, and everywhere smelt like berries.

"This doesn't bother you, does it, girls?"

Beverly's mother hated blueberries because she ate so many of them in Labrador when she was a kid. Her family used to pick them in empty margarine containers and eat them for breakfast, lunch, and dinner.

"It's fine," her mother said, and Beverly thought it was nice that her mother was lying to her father to make him happy. Beverly thought her father's smoking was starting to worry them all now that he was sixty.

"All these celebrities are dying really young," Beverly said while she flipped through an *Us Weekly*. "Like, in their sixties."

"Since when do you care about celebrities?" her father asked.

Beverly thought it was funny that her parents always concerned themselves with the wrong thing. They cared more about her earring than her chipped tooth. They were more worried about her thinking of celebrities than death.

"I'm going over to Steve's," Beverly said.

"Have fun!" her mother responded. "Tell Denise and Brian we say hello."

Beverly's connection to Steve felt almost biological. Their moms had been in the same new mom group and when they were old enough would take the kids to the YMCA so they could party on the weekends. Her father inhaled his vape and Beverly heard him coughing enormously as she closed the door behind her. He still wasn't used to the change.

On her way over to Steve's, he messaged her and called her toothless. He said LOL after though, so Beverly would know he was joking. He asked her to bring snacks and told her he would see her soon. Steve's family lived in a big house on Waterford Bridge Road with lots of trees in the back. They had a tree house that he and his brothers had built when they were kids and Beverly's parents used to have to pull her out of it by the ankles.

Beverly met Steve in the tree house and hit her head on a branch she had always been too small to notice. She'd brought Purity cookies and Steve ate two really quick. She was wearing a pink dress she had bought at the thrift store with green bike shorts underneath. She sat cross-legged in the tree house and ate a Purity cookie. The crumbs from the cookie fell onto her chest and she laughed.

"Did you put lipstick on?" Steve asked.

"I don't know, just like gloss or whatever."

"It looks good." He was looking at her like he wanted to say something. But she knew he wouldn't. He would never do anything that would make her feel uncomfortable. He was thoughtful and smart and he wanted her to be happy.

"What do you want to do next year?" Beverly asked. She'd been avoiding talking about it because she knew he was avoiding thinking about it.

"I don't want to talk about it." He ate a cookie. "I'm sorry."

"That's okay, you don't have to talk about it."

"I feel like everybody has it all figured out and I just don't, yet. I feel like leaving Newfoundland is hard and weird and everything else is connected. I just want to be here, in this tree fort with you."

"I think that's nice and okay." Steve moved closer to her and put his hands on her thighs. His hands felt familiar even though he had never touched her like this before. He kissed her on the mouth and when he pulled away he had pink lip gloss on. Beverly giggled and tilted her head to the side.

"Is this okay?" he asked.

She nodded with her mouth closed and he kissed her again with tongue. She felt his tongue find hers through the hole in her front tooth. She could taste the Purity cookie in his teeth and everything felt familiar.

Rebecca gave Beverly the part of Eve and said that she wanted to watch her be tempted. Ginny was playing Satan and they were rehearsing the part where Satan turns into a snake to tempt Eve to eat the apple. They were in the Holy Heart theatre and Rebecca was wearing a red beret. Rebecca started talking incessantly about her childhood and how she thought growing up she would be an actress. She said her mother pushed back against it but then emphasized that her mother didn't understand her and her big dreams for a future in Hollywood. Beverly turned to Ginny and asked her quietly if she thought Rebecca was maybe just a run-of-the-mill narcissist.

"Ginny, now, please slither across the stage on your stomach," Rebecca ordered.

"But this is a new shirt is the thing," Ginny said.

Beverly laughed but part of her felt bad for her friend.

"Ginny, I'm not gonna ask you again. Get down on your stomach."

Ginny had her arms crossed in defiance. She chuckled, still pretending she thought it was funny, but Beverly saw a tear leak out of her right eye with the eyeliner wave on the side.

After rehearsal, Beverly held Ginny until she stopped crying and convinced her that playing Satan was really an honour. "He's really a fallen angel," Beverly said. "I mean it, it's a layered and troubled character."

On Friday night, Rebecca had all the girls from the play over to her house to discuss plot. She rented a narrow house on Colonial that was painted yellow and orange. Bookshelves covered every wall of the living room and she'd put out cheese plates. Beverly wore a black dress and Vans and drank one of the non-alcoholic spritzers Rebecca had laid out beside the cheese. She looked through the photos on the fireplace and for the first time, she noticed Rebecca was pretty. Her hair was dark and curly and always thrown up haphazardly and she had glasses with yellow frames. There were a lot of pictures of her with a man who looked older. They had gone to Niagara Falls and Parliament together and taken pictures with a selfie stick. Beverly wondered who this man was. Rebecca never wore a wedding ring and besides, it kind of seemed like she hated men.

"Who is this?" Beverly asked.

"That's my husband," Rebecca said as she joined Beverly in the living room.

"I didn't know you were married."

"Why would you?"

"I don't know. I mean, I guess I wouldn't."

Rebecca took a sip of red wine from a stemmed glass with a chip on the rim.

"I mean, I think about it sometimes. What you guys are like outside of school and like if you're in a relationship and stuff," Beverly said.

"Yeah, I don't want that. I don't want you to judge me in relation to a man. That's why I get you to call me Rebecca."

"I wouldn't judge you."

"You wouldn't mean to, but people still think this way, Beverly. You have to know that."

"Is that why you're not allowing men in the Garden of Eden?" Beverly sipped her fake wine spritzer and spilled some of it on her chin.

"I don't want all Adam's traits in the play to be considered masculine traits." Rebecca paused when Beverly looked confused. "I want love and heroism and sacrifice to be feminine qualities too. I don't want the first man, the one with power over all of creation, to be the one to sacrifice for a woman. I want it to be the other way around."

Beverly leaned against the kitchen counter and put her spritzer down. "Well, can you just do that? This is Milton's story, not yours."

"If I don't change this for women then this is always going to be the reality. That the woman is the dumb, vain one who is so easily convinced to eat the apple and her boyfriend loves her so much that he will just eat it too. And he's the one who gets the credit. I'm just tired of men getting the credit!" Rebecca's voice was getting louder and the girls from the living room were looking in with spritzers in their tiny hands. "Don't you want women to get the credit, Beverly?"

Beverly stared at Rebecca. "I think you're being dramatic," she said. She immediately regretted saying this, but she could see the weakness and the flimsiness behind a lot of Rebecca's ideas. She didn't believe her. It seemed like Rebecca might be pushing back against traditional ideas of men and the family because of some larger insecurity she wasn't sharing.

"I just don't want you to be tempted by men, Beverly. You're too good for that. You're too smart."

"Thank you," Beverly whispered, like her being smart was a secret between them. Something in Rebecca's eyes assured her that this was much bigger than the play. Rebecca was acting out in an effort to convince herself that her ordinary life was as valuable as the fame she'd longed for growing up. Beverly would make an effort to be nicer to Rebecca and her ideas. She started to think about Steve and him kissing her in the tree house behind his mother's garden. She thought about him sliding his hands up her thighs and asking her if it was okay. He was different. He didn't want the credit, he just wanted her.

Beverly pushed past Rebecca and said, "C'mon, let's talk about Paradise."

Beverly sat beside Ginny on the couch and squeezed her leg. There were ten girls there, all of them drinking spritzers. Beverly ate a piece of cheese, which was a terrible combination.

"So, Beverly and Ginny, how do you think we should do the seduction scene?" Rebecca began. When neither answered, she continued. "Satan is disguised as the snake and he seduces Eve with his rhetoric. He gets her to eat the apple by preying on her vanity."

Beverly's face turned red like everyone had figured her out. Like everyone thought she could be tempted.

"Why does it even matter if she eats the apple?" Tracy Doyle asked.

"God gave them one rule. They can't eat from the tree of knowledge, or they're punished by death," Beverly said.

"Satan wants to poison them."

"Why, though?" Tracy asked.

"Because he's jealous of their love. Because he's a bad person. I don't know, he's miserable! He's Satan."

After they left Rebecca's, they walked to Ryan's house. He was having a party while his parents were away in Fogo. His mother had been accepted to do an artist residency and would be gone until the summer. The girls walked down Gower Street and the red light from Halliday's lit up their shoes.

"I got into MUN," Ginny whispered as she kicked a rock down the street, a little further each time.

"What! That's great!"

"Is it?"

"Yes! Of course," Beverly responded. Ginny hadn't gotten into her top two schools, TMU and Queen's, and she desperately wanted to leave Newfoundland. She had come to Beverly's university acceptance party and eaten her cake so fast she got the hiccups.

"Ginny, come on. You'll love it. You can live in residence or just move out and you'll like never have to see your parents."

They walked into Halliday's and the bell over the door chimed like a church. Ginny bought two sour keys for twenty-five cents each and handed one to Beverly. As they walked down the hill toward Duckworth, Beverly could see the top of Cabot Tower. She remembered a few years back when Steve thought it would be a good idea to go to the top of Signal Hill on Halloween. Beverly was dressed as a ghost because she couldn't think of a costume, so at the last minute she cut a hole in a pillowcase. Steve was dressed as a slice of pepperoni pizza. Ginny was wearing a tiara and her hair was all over the place in the wind. When they got to the top, some of the guys started jumping off the cannon. Beverly told Steve to stop, that he was scaring her. He told her he was just going to jump one last time and then he tripped. The last thing Beverly saw was a large piece of pizza rolling down Signal Hill. Ginny turned around and threw her arms around Beverly's neck dramatically like it could have been bad. But when they looked down the hill, Steve was lying just twenty feet away, his roll stopped by a rock. He got up and dusted the slice of pizza off and screamed that he was fine, but they were right, he probably shouldn't do that again.

When Beverly asked Ginny if she remembered that time, Ginny swallowed her sour key and said, "Yeah, the fall of man." This made Beverly laugh.

When they got to Ryan's house on Prescott they added their Vans to a pile of Vans that were all the same, just different sizes. In the kitchen, Steve and a guy named Anthony Marshall held Ryan upside down over a keg of beer. His dirty white socks left a grey mark on his parents' kitchen ceiling and he stumbled when they put him down. He pulled Ginny toward him and kissed her on the mouth. Steve smiled at Beverly and handed her a can of India. She smiled, revealing the cap on her tooth.

"Hey, I can't see your brain anymore," he whispered when

she was beside him. "How was Rebecca's?"

Beverly said it was fine but she thought that Ginny was mad because she was Satan. The boys had brought Ryan's ping-pong table up from the basement and they had set red cups up like pyramids on either side.

Ryan chugged his beer and said to Steve, "C'mon, you and your girl versus me and mine."

Beverly resented being called someone's girl but she agreed to play anyway. It was a game that people seemed to be better at the more they had to drink. Beverly looked to the side as Steve was about to shoot and she saw that he had a drop of sweat coming down off his hairline like water. She thought about their baptism and how they'd always done things together. Beverly sank the winning shot into Ginny's cup. Seeing Ginny's face fall, Beverly immediately wished she had just let Ginny win at something for once.

After ten, the party started to fill up until there were people Beverly didn't recognize, which almost never happened in St. John's. Steve had been holding Beverly's hand since beer pong and she felt tethered but also free. She thought about her earlier conversation with Rebecca. God had given Adam and Eve total freedom but not freedom from each other.

Beverly left Steve to go to the bathroom and stopped in a bedroom at the top of the staircase. Ginny was in there with two girls from their class and they were stick-and-poking an angel tattoo onto Ginny's ankle.

"What the hell are you doing?" Beverly asked, suddenly feeling drunk.

"I'm getting a tattoo," Ginny yelled. "Something permanent."

"Why?"

"I don't know, so I can remind myself that I'm not the devil!"

"Stop it. If you read the play or listened to Rebecca, you would know that Satan is a fallen angel."

"Okay, so I'm both then." Ginny stopped talking and winced with pain. "Not all of us can be Eve, Beverly."

"That's not fair."

"NOTHING IS FAIR!" Ginny screamed so loudly that the other girl, Trish, messed up the tattoo.

"What is wrong with you?" Beverly asked, still standing in the doorway.

"Just get out, Beverly."

Beverly left and slammed the door after her. She knew Ginny was acting erratically because she was drunk. When she got to the washroom, she realized she had gotten her period. She searched the cupboards and found one of Ryan's mother's tampons. Back downstairs she quickly found Steve and told him she wanted to get drunk too.

Steve put his hand on her arm. "What's wrong? Are you okay?"

"Yeah, I'm fine. I just want to get drunk."

He looked at her like he was worried but he agreed. He pulled a huge bottle of green apple Smirnoff out of the freezer and poured her a shot reluctantly. People were elbowing her in the back and she felt hot and crowded.

"I'm worried about you," he said.

"Don't be worried about me. I'm fine. I don't need you to be looking out for me all the time. I'm my own person."

She slurred the last part of the statement and Steve said, "What?"

"I'm my own person," she slurred again. Beverly walked away with the bottle of vodka and had conversations with people she knew she wouldn't remember having. In the backyard, she could feel Steve talking to someone behind her like he was a part of everything she did. She was talking to Ryan about her tooth and he pulled her lip up toward the sky and said, "Bev, your tooth looks sick. That was gnarly when that shit chipped."

"Yeah, I know, and I just feel like I had this hole in my head, you know. And I'm like, what is going to fill this hole? Kind of like the pool, you know when we went the other night." She could feel herself rambling but thought she was making perfect sense. "Like when they emptied out the water and they replaced it with new stuff. Like I just don't know who is going to fill the hole in my head. Also I forget, did I leave the tooth at the pool?"

Ryan started laughing and Steve joined in the conversation, looking at her like he was disappointed. Beverly was swinging the vodka bottle in the air like she was conducting something, she just didn't know what yet.

"I have your tooth," Steve said, and Beverly pointed the vodka bottle at him like she would a gun.

"You have my tooth?" she slurred, but she did have a distant memory of him pocketing it. "So you can fill the hole in my head."

At that moment, Ginny barged out of the back door with blood dripping from her ankle. Her eyes looked hollow in a way that made Beverly nervous. "Your ankle is bleeding," Beverly said and for a second she thought about her period. Ryan put his arm around Ginny so tightly it looked almost violent.

Ginny put out her palm and said, "Look what I have." There were four plastic pills with white powder inside. "I bought them from this guy named Buddy upstairs."

"Buddy? What is this, a Salinger book?"

Steve was the only one that laughed and Beverly appreciated it.

"C'mon. You down?" Ginny said.

"No, I'm not down." Beverly said, mocking her, which she didn't mind doing, given that she was still hurt about the tattoo.

"Steve?" Ginny said.

"No. Thank you." Steve was eyeing Beverly and she could feel it like a heat against her face. She wished he would stop looking at her like she was his whole world. Beverly looked beside her and noticed Ryan's mother's herb garden. Steve leaned in and whispered in her ear, "I'm going to get you a glass of water."

"Beverly, come on. You deserve this." Ginny was looking at her with that wave on her eye. She had her dark hair pulled back in a low ponytail and she looked nice. "You've spent all year getting these good marks. You're moving soon and you have this huge scholarship. C'mon, you have nothing to lose." Ginny was holding the pills so close to Beverly they were almost touching her. Beverly ran her tongue along her teeth and her mouth tasted like an apple.

"I don't think it's a good idea. I'm not supposed to do this. My parents would kill me."

"They want you to do this. They just say they don't because they want you to be independent. But they want you to have experiences. They want you to have fun!"

"I don't think that makes sense."

"C'mon. Yes it does. It'll be fun! We'll just have a good time with each other, before you go."

Beverly felt confused and upset. Rebecca told her never to be tempted; her best friend was being a snake. She took the pill and popped it open so the white powder fell into her hand like concealer. Ginny was smiling big like she had finally won. Steve, who had come back with the glass of water, was standing in the doorway as Ginny licked the powder off her own hand. Steve looked at Beverly like he didn't know her and she thought it was the first time that had happened. The bottle of vodka suddenly slipped out of her hand and smashed beside Ryan's mother's garden. Everything started to smell like apples.

"Give me one," Steve said to Ginny as he walked toward them. He put the glass of water he had gotten for Beverly on the ground beside the smashed glass.

"No, Steve, don't do it if you don't want to," Beverly said.

"If you're going to do it, then so am I," Steve said loudly as he turned around to face her.

"Dude, chill out," Ryan said from a chair on the corner of the back porch.

Beverly looked at Steve as he licked the drugs off his hand.

"If something bad happens, at least it'll happen to both of us."

Beverly roamed around the party. At some point she lost her phone and also her track of time. She met Buddy and asked him if his parents liked Salinger. She moved her jaw back and forth and forward and back and she worried about her tooth. She found herself in the bedroom at the top of the stairs, the one Ginny had been in earlier when she had become a permanent angel. She lay down on the bed and decided almost immediately that she was in Ryan's room. He had a Pro Skates poster on his ceiling and a lava lamp on the bedside table. His sheets were blue plaid and her skin tingled against them. She climbed underneath the sheets and started to cry. She felt impulsive and sad that she had lost control. She was facing the wall when she heard the door open and when she turned around Steve was there.

"What's wrong?" he asked softly like he didn't want to hurt her. For a second she forgot he was high because he looked perfect.

"I'm sorry I was mean to you earlier."

She felt her tears falling sideways off her face and onto Ryan's pillow. Steve crawled into bed beside her. "You don't have to be sorry. I'm just protective of you." He wiped tears off her face with the pad of his thumb and it felt good.

"How are you feeling? Do you feel high?"

"Yeah. But it's weird. I'm just trying to decide what it even feels like."

"I think it feels really good to have people touch you," Beverly said.

Steve leaned in and kissed her. It was overwhelming and confusing, like it was completely consuming her. She ran her nails through his hair and felt him moan into her mouth. It seemed unbelievable, getting to see someone you know everything about do things you've never seen. Steve kissed her neck and then her cheek and her ear, which still hurt where she got it pierced. He moved on top of her and said, "Is this okay?"

"Stop asking me if things are okay," Beverly whispered. Instead of feeling things in small touches, she was feeling everything at once. She thought she was still crying but she couldn't be sure.

"I'm sorry. I just don't want to do anything you don't want to do."

Beverly grabbed each side of Steve's head and looked at him. "I can't stop crying." She wiped her eyes and moved Steve so he was beside her on the bed. "I'm just feeling too much at once."

"You know I've loved you forever, right?"

"I have known that, yes," she said.

"Your mouth tastes like an apple."

"Yeah, it's the vodka." Beverly kissed him. "You know, after Adam and Eve fell from the Garden of Eden, they had sex."

"I don't want to have sex while you're crying."

Beverly smiled and said, "I don't either."

"Your pupils are really big right now." She felt a weird compulsion to touch his eyeball, to know what it felt like. Instead she turned away from him and he wrapped his arms around her in Ryan's bed. He put his hand on her stomach and talked about how he wanted to climb into her belly button and never leave. And then he said, "I can feel your ribs."

Beverly met Steve at his tree house the next day and brought Purity cookies again. He was sitting cross-legged on a pillow with dinosaurs, reading *Paradise Lost*.

"I wanted to see how it ends before opening night," he said.

"I've been puking all morning." Beverly was wearing jean shorts and an Iron Maiden shirt that she had stolen from

Ryan's drawer before going home. Her uterus was cramping so much she couldn't stand straight. She sat down and crossed her legs like Steve.

"Have you talked to Ginny?" Steve asked while he ate a cookie.

"No. I'm still mad at her. I don't know, she didn't even seem like herself. I felt like she just used everything she knows about me to betray me. She tricked me."

"She's jealous of you, Bev. You have to know that."

Beverly ate a cookie and it made her want to puke. "I wish I could feel pure again."

"It's going to be okay."

"I feel guilty."

"So does Eve," Steve said, pointing at the book open at the spine beside them. "After she eats the apple."

Beverly laughed and said, "You read it."

"I'm almost done but I have to go to Costco for my dad. Do you want to come?"

"Yeah sure! But only if we can eat samples in every aisle."

Beverly started manoeuvring out of the tree house. She jumped from the last plank of wood on the tree and waited for Steve on the ground. He threw her his copy of *Paradise Lost* right before he tripped on the top plank of wood. His body hit the ground hard as he fell into his mother's tulips.

"Jesus, Steve." Beverly ran toward him and told him not to move. "I'm going to get your parents, okay. Don't move, okay, are you listening to me?" She could feel tears leaving her eyes and was convinced her constitution was weakened right now by her hangover. Steve's parents rushed out and surrounded him like a fire and called an ambulance. When the paramedics got there they put Steve on an orange stretcher and ran the stretcher through his mother's garden, crushing her succulents.

"We're concerned he may have broken a rib," one paramedic said.

Beverly let out a noise that sounded like something between a laugh and a snort. Steve's parents and Beverly rode in the ambulance with him and Beverly held one of Steve's hands and his mother held the other. In Beverly's other hand was Steve's copy of *Paradise Lost*.

"Bev," Steve said quietly.

"Baby, don't talk if it hurts," his mother urged, pushing Steve's hair back off his forehead.

"Bev, tell me what happens at the end of the story."

"They find paradise in each other."

STARS

When I told my mother I was gay she threw an egg at me. It cracked right in the middle of my forehead and dripped down into my facial hair and onto my lips so I could taste it. My mother used to play baseball for Newfoundland and she pitched a good game.

When I was eight she told me I was getting thick in the hips and then she pointed so I would know where she meant. I started losing weight by eating my meals differently. I had read in *In Touch* magazine that stars were eating six small meals a day as opposed to three big ones. A couple of years after I changed my diet my father suggested we go to California as a family. He wanted to check out the Hollywood sign, Griffith Observatory and Sunset Boulevard. He couldn't stop talking about it. When we got there, my father took a photo of me sitting cross-legged on the A at LAX. He made a comment about how the letter matched my name, Adam.

In California, the sun was so hot I had to wear a visor. We went to the studio where they filmed the TV show *Friends* and we sat in the live audience with numbers hanging from our necks. I personally thought *Friends* was a bit homophobic but my father thought it was a hoot.

That night I held my mother's hand as we walked down Sunset Boulevard and stomped on the stars of celebrities. I was walking all over Robert De Niro when she asked me if I was happy.

"I don't know, Mom. I'm ten."

"Yeah, but you must know. Like what do you think about all day? Do things scare you?" She paused on Barbra Streisand. "I just don't feel that we're as close as we used to be."

I wanted to tell her that we weren't as close because she had sabotaged the relationship by treating me like an adult. I didn't know anyone else who had a mother like mine and it seemed that I loved her too much to make it stop.

Before we left LA, we went to the studio that looked like a neighbourhood in New York. You could walk the streets and pretend you were in the Big Apple. There were men zipping all around us on little carts like in the airport. They were there to patrol our behaviour.

"Are we in LA or New York?" my father said as he climbed some steps to a fake brownstone.

My mother and I didn't laugh. Usually we felt the same way toward him. We loved him at the same times and hated him at the same times. I put my hand in my father's hand and encouraged him to join us in fake Greenwich Village. I walked in between them and I felt small.

Back at the hotel that night, when my father began his snoring, my mother looked over at me in the double bed parallel to theirs. "You know, I've never felt as close to anyone as I feel to you."

"Thank you, Mom." It was like she was waiting for me to say it back. But I was feeling far away from the things I knew. I couldn't be sure that any way I felt in LA was the right way because nothing seemed real enough to be right.

The next day we went to see the Hollywood sign. My dad wore a huge camera around his neck like a rosary and I thought he looked ridiculous. We walked up the hiking trail in single file with my mother at the front. She was always the most competitive. I could hear her breathing heavily and I wondered if she missed being an athlete. When I turned around to find my father, he pointed his camera at me and told me to smile.

"We're going to want this memory. Trust me."

I rolled my eyes and knew my mother was probably rolling hers too. When we got to the Griffith Observatory, my father encouraged us to go further. He wanted us to reach the Hollywood sign. He wanted to take a picture of me on the O. My father led the line this time, to the Hollywood sign, a trail I was pretty sure was off limits. When we got there, he started talking about structure and how looking at this word, Hollywood, had become a sensation he didn't understand.

"It's like a reminder of where you are, Dad. People want to know that they are somewhere special. People need to be reminded that they're famous and rich. So they look up and they see this and it makes them breathe easier. They're a star."

My mother put me in a headlock after I said this and ruffled my hair. She gave me a boost and I climbed onto the O and stood in the middle. My father took a photo of me that was too close up so it just looked the same as the one he took at the airport.

"A-okay," my father said as we headed back.

When I was younger, my father would tuck me in and tell me the story of how he had met my mother. While he talked, I would stare at the plastic stars my mother and I had glued on my ceiling when I was four. She had put me on her shoulders and I could feel how strong she was. My father's story of how he met her was different every time, but some details stayed the same. He had gone to see her play at a field in CBS when they were freshmen and he remembered that her right arm was bigger than her left. After the game, he'd wandered across the pitch with his hands in his pockets. When he got close, he could see that she had sweat dripping down her cheek like tears. He always made sure to tell me this part because no one had ever seen my mother cry. He told her she impressed him and this made her blush.

My father is an architect. His office has high ceilings and a woman who sits at a desk with her hair twisted in the back like a dinner roll. He builds luxury condominiums and there's talk of one going up by the water, almost right down in the Battery. I think this would be a sin because it would block the view of the Narrows but my father says it would be great for the family.

When my father got home that night, we didn't talk about the egg. Instead my father talked about a new project at work and how they had to build new urination infrastructure for dogs. "Everyone at the office is interested in using space differently," he said.

My mother stuck a Brussels sprout in her mouth and when it was too hot she spit it out. She didn't think anyone noticed, but I noticed almost everything she did. My father was going on about how young architects these days wanted new room for play, they wanted space to be more than it had been in the past, they wanted to be better than they had been before. He talked about vertical space and how soon everyone would be living in condos. My father would go on these rants and usually my mother and I would let him. And the longer he talked, the stronger the feeling was that we were in something together, the three of us. My mother always seemed much stronger than my father. She didn't let things bother her in the same way. This is why I was surprised by the egg. I thought I knew her. I thought I'd cracked her.

I was seeing a guy named Finn who had recently moved from Toronto. He was hired as a line cook at the restaurant where I was a server. The restaurant was new and the lighting was low. Whenever I was running food I would look up and meet his eyes. He asked me to go to the new Boston Pizza on Friday and I met him there for drinks. We sat in a booth meant for a large party and Finn put his feet up beside me. I was distracted by the wall of TVs behind him playing a variety of sports and news channels. Finn talked about how Memorial had a really good geology program and the tuition was cheap. But he had never been to Newfoundland before and he had already seen all the same people twice.

"I don't know, when I was younger I wanted to be a star," Finn said.

I watched a red-carpet event play behind his right ear and I told him about when my parents took me to LA. "It was weird. My dad is an architect and he was just like obsessed with the Hollywood sign. We have pictures of me posing on all these different things and like walking on Hollywood Boulevard."

Finn was sipping a grape martini but I ordered a beer.

"That's awesome," he said.

"Yeah, it just didn't feel real or whatever. It was all so fake.

All the stardom." Finn leaned forward and kissed me on the mouth. I had never kissed anyone before other than my mother and I felt terrified that someone might see me and finally figure me out. Finn wiped his thumb across my bottom lip and it made my whole body shiver like it did sometimes when I was cold.

"What do you do besides work at the restaurant?" he asked when he pulled away.

"I paint a bit," I said. Finn smiled and nodded like it made sense that I would do that. "I don't really know how good it all is but I'm thinking of maybe applying to Grenfell for next fall."

"I'd love to see you paint sometime," he said. He put his elbow on the table and leaned closer to me. I wanted him to kiss me again and then wipe it off after.

Finn and I started going to places we thought no one would see us. He had moved into a two-bedroom place above International Flavours and he wanted to repaint. He had paint chips hanging from different walls of his apartment that he had left there with thumbtacks. I didn't know which colours worked best.

"Maybe just leave the paint chips there. I like how they go from light to dark, it's like you're getting all those colours and you don't have choose."

"No, I want to choose," he said.

So we went to the Walmart on Kelsey Drive and he kissed me and put his hand on my ribs while the lady searched for a seafoam green Finn wanted for his bathroom. He went and looked at appliances and light fixtures while I went to buy gummy worms in the value pack. As we walked back out to his car he squeezed my hand until it hurt. I hopped on the end of his cart full of paint and he pushed the cart really fast and started running until I felt like I had no control. It was scary but I was laughing like I was happy. Ever since I was young, I've always loved Walmart. I would get a small cart and push it beside my mother's big one. I liked it because we could get everything at once: groceries and plants and clothes, all piled up in the cart until she didn't have any more room.

When we got back to Finn's place we lugged the cans of paint behind International Flavours and up the stairs into his house. Finn was hungry so we went down to eat at the restaurant. We drank water out of red party cups and Finn talked about how it was his favourite restaurant because he could have both chicken and lamb at once.

When we went back upstairs, I saw that his bedroom was still empty, with just a red sleeping bag on the ground. He took his shirt off to change into one with holes and no sleeves. When he began to undress, I walked up behind him and kissed him on the neck. He smelled like sweat and Mennen Speed Stick. The hair on his chin tickled my cheek as I put my hands on his waist right above his brown leather belt. I felt him flinch and it made me wonder if he was nervous too.

He put on the shirt with holes and opened the can of paint by loosening the lid all around the edges. He handed me a brush and said, "Show me what you got, champ."

I realized he wanted me to paint because I had told him I was a painter. But I had never shown anyone my work before and it felt personal and important.

"Oh, that's okay, I'm not very good," I said as I turned away from him.

"Dude, just paint something. It's fine, it's not going to be there forever."

Finn went to the kitchen and boiled some water for tea and when he came back he leaned in the doorway of the bedroom with his arms crossed. He took large bites of a ham sandwich with mustard and said, "Is that your mom?"

The painting was my mother with one leg in front and the other one behind. She was standing on a base and she had a ball in her hand, or maybe it was an egg. She was pitching something.

"That's really good, man," Finn said.

"When I told my mom I was gay, she threw an egg at my head."

"I'm sorry that happened to you."

"I really didn't expect it."

Finn approached me and grabbed the brush from my hand. He dipped it into the paint and started to paint over it. I hugged him from behind and thanked him for covering it up.

That night over dinner, my father talked about how two floors had been added to his condo on the water. My mother had made shepherd's pie for dinner and the ratios were all off.

"How's the restaurant?" my father asked me and a piece of potato left his mouth like a word.

"It's okay. We started making a new kind of tartar sauce for the fish and chips." I looked at my mother, who looked positively bored. I hadn't told them about Finn and I felt good about something still being mine. "I'm thinking of applying to school."

"Honey, that's great," my mother said, suddenly interested.

"What are you planning to do, son?" My father wiped his

mouth with his napkin and crossed his legs.

"Well, I think I'm going to apply to Grenfell for a BFA."

"Interesting, interesting," my father said like he was considering a proposal at work. "Maybe you'll keep thinking about it for a while?"

I wanted to tell him that his condo was blocking something special and that painting was creating space too. I wanted to tell him I was gay and things weren't always how they appeared.

When I got to my room, I watched Netflix. Lately I had to have it on to fall asleep. Sometimes I watched old movies with my favourite Hollywood stars, but usually I just watched *The Office* and felt myself getting tired. The familiarity of it made me feel happy, like I could depend on it.

The 2017 Briar was in St. John's and I took Finn to a draw. His eighteenth birthday had been the week before and I thought we should celebrate. When we arrived, I bought us a large poutine and the gravy leaked out of the bottom and made our hands smell. My mother had always been really into curling. She had spent all week bundled up on the sofa with a crocheted blanket wrapped around her feet. She got excited about most televised sports but she really loved curling. She liked the precision of it, the banality of it. I thought about taking her to the live game instead of Finn but I still felt hurt about the egg. I remembered the texture of it running down my face.

Finn and I sat right by the announcer's booth and we could hear them analyzing the game above us. Our seats were sticky from the spilt drinks of previous games and I grabbed Finn's hand and told him I was excited. Eight teams played at once; it was hard to focus. The curlers all looked smaller than they did on TV and when I said this to Finn, he told me stars always looked smaller in person.

"It's weird, I've been like watching these men curl since I was a kid."

"That's so weird. My parents think curling is so fucking boring," Finn said and took a slug of a Black Horse we were sharing.

"These people are like celebrities to me or something." I scanned the crowd for people I knew. I wanted to tell Finn that the idea of celebrity always excited me and made me think about things outside of myself and outside of Newfoundland. I wanted to tell him I watched every red carpet. I wanted to tell him that I always thought I would be famous. "I think my mom gets really sad when she sees stuff like this happen in Newfoundland. You know, she almost made it pro. Her coaches set her up with scholarships and stuff and she had a full ride to the University of Texas and then she threw out her shoulder." I took a sip of the beer. "And she met my dad, and that was it." The crowd cheered and stood up when Team Newfoundland won the end. People rang cowbells and swung Newfoundland flags in the air. One half of the stadium screamed Newfoundland and the other half screamed Labrador, like a question and answer. "It's weird to think about her making it big," I said.

"It sounds like you and your mom are really close," Finn answered. "Have you told her about me?"

"No. She hurt my feelings so much I don't want to tell her anything important now."

The fries turned cold and the cheese curds fell to the side of the tray. Newfoundland drew to the button in the final end, and the crowd lost their minds. A woman in front of me cried until her shoulders fell forward.

We left Mile One holding hands and walked all the way down Duckworth and went down the stairs by the Ship. As we approached Water Street, I saw my dad's condo.

"You know, you used to be able to see all the way past the Narrows. Sometimes on a really nice day I would sit down here and plan my escape from Newfoundland by swimming as far as I could go."

"Your dad has nice taste," Finn said, pointing to the condo.

"That's not the point," I told him. I looked up and I could see the stars. I told Finn I thought they were beautiful.

"You can't see the stars in Toronto with all the garbage and shit in the air, and all those new buildings," Finn said.

We walked past Raymonds all the way to the Four Sisters before we climbed the hill to Finn's place. He was still holding my hand and even though both of our hands felt sweaty, neither of us let go. As we turned the corner where Quidi Vidi Road meets Duckworth, when Finn's house was finally in sight, a car drove by slowly with two guys hanging out the back window. One guy was holding an open carton of large white eggs. The eggs came toward us faster than we could duck and when one hit my head I immediately saw my mother's face—her kind eyes and the smile I loved.

ACKNOWLEDGEMENTS

Thank you to Lisa Moore for encouraging me to stay in St. John's and write. Nothing like this ever could have happened without you.

Thank you to the MUN English Department for giving me space, time, and money to write these stories. To Joel Deshaye and Jennifer Lokash for being so competent. And to Danine Farquharson for giving me every answer and being my friend.

Support from the Banff Centre for the Arts, the Newfoundland and Labrador Arts Council, and the City of St. John's allowed me to finish writing this collection. I'm so fortunate to live in St. John's, where I feel supported and held all the time.

Thank you to Rebecca, Rhonda, Nicole, George, and everyone at Breakwater Books for your care with putting this book out into the world. To my editor Kate Kennedy, who knew exactly what I needed. And to Claire Wilkshire, whom I trust immensely.

To Megan Gail Coles, Carmella Gray-Cosgrove, Lisa Moore, and Craig Francis Power for offering blurbs of this book. I hope to write like you all one day.

To Ethan Murphy for being such a curious force and such a good friend to me—I feel so lucky to have this image as my cover.

When I wrote this book, I was living with Noah Bender and Jim McEwen, both of whom taught me so much about how to live and document this weird life. I'm thankful to everyone at Kimberly Row, Chapel Street, and Fixed for the fun and the chaos. To my best friends, Colleen Daly, Becky Gibson, Amelia Harris, Isobel McKenna, Nico Paulo, Catherine Roberge, Amery Sandford and Isha Watson, who tell me the best stories. Thank you, Drew Wolfson Bell, the original soft serve lover.

Thanks to my grandparents, Velma and Revelin, for showing me how to make art and be creative. And to Kay for being the smartest one in the room.

Thanks to my parents, Olive and Papa, who have always encouraged my drama. You've given me the best life.

ALLISON GRAVES received her BA in English literature from Dalhousie University and her MA in creative writing from Memorial University, where she wrote this collection of short stories. Her fiction has won *Room* magazine's annual fiction contest and the Newfoundland Arts and Letters Award. She is the current fiction editor of *Riddle Fence*. She is doing a PhD at Memorial and likes to play drums and climb Signal Hill. Allison lives in St. John's, Newfoundland and Labrador.